BOOTS AND PIECES

BOOTS AND PIECES

By Emily Ecton

To Mayla —
It was fun talking
to you.
Emily Ecton

ALADDIN PAPERBACKS
NEW YORK   LONDON   TORONTO   SYDNEY

*To my parents, Hank and Barbara, who told me
that the first book has to be dedicated to your parents.
That's true, right? (Right?)*

This book is a work of fiction. Any references to historical events, real people,
or real locales are used fictitiously. Other names, characters, places, and
incidents are the product of the author's imagination, and any resemblance to
actual events or locales or persons, living or dead, is entirely coincidental.

☙ ALADDIN PAPERBACKS

An imprint of Simon & Schuster Children's Publishing Division

1230 Avenue of the Americas, New York, NY 10020

Copyright © 2008 by Emily Ecton

All rights reserved, including the right of reproduction in whole or
in part in any form.

ALADDIN PAPERBACKS and related logo are registered trademarks of
Simon & Schuster, Inc.

Designed by Lisa Vega

The text of this book was set in Bembo.

Manufactured in the United States of America

First Aladdin Paperbacks edition August 2008

10 9 8 7 6 5 4 3 2 1

Library of Congress Control Number 2007940697

ISBN-13: 978-1-4169-6167-3

ISBN-10: 1-4169-6167-4

CHAPTER 1

IF TY HADN'T KICKED ME IN THE HEAD THAT DAY, I probably wouldn't even have noticed when Stacy Sizemore disappeared. Heck, nobody else really seemed to, not at first anyway. Not until they found the pieces.

We were out in my front yard after school, just fooling around, practicing our karate moves. Not that either one of us takes karate. The karate teacher down at Jazzercise quit to open a lube shop three counties over. But we weren't about to let that stop us—I mean, we watch kung fu on TV all the time. What's to know?

Apparently a lot, because I'd barely even settled on a kung fu pose before Ty jumped up and kicked me right in the forehead. I have to admit, it was a great shot. I couldn't appreciate it right then, though, since I was busy keeling over and nearly cracking my skull on Tootie, Mom's plastic garden duck. I was glad Tootie survived, but I couldn't even begin to do that "I'm okay" routine to make Ty feel better. Heck, Tootie was lucky she didn't end up wearing the SpaghettiOs I had for lunch. It hurt that bad.

It was right about then that Stacy Sizemore came trotting out of her house. I say trotting because she had on her favorite pink heels—the three-inch ones with the bow on the front that make her take funny little baby steps. There I was, writhing in agony, and what does Stacy do? Without a word, Stacy Sizemore just steps over my head and staggers into her car, leaving me on the ground choking in a cloud of her cheap perfume. Isn't that great? She wasn't even that careful about it. I'm serious—I could've lost an ear.

I'm actually surprised I didn't; that's the kind of thing that would happen to me. Years from now I'd be on the senior superlatives page in the yearbook, next to the kids voted Class Clown, Most Popular, Most Likely to Succeed—you know, the good ones. And there I'd be, Arlene Jacobs, plain kid, brown hair, missing that ear, voted Most Likely to Lose Another Body Part. And my class quote would be, "Gee, thanks, Stacy."

So when she turned up missing the next day, I took particular interest. Okay, maybe it was part gloating—a see-what-happens-when-you-step-on-my-hair type of thing. (Because she totally stepped on my hair when I was lying on the sidewalk.) But I'm sure a little of it was real friendly concern.

At least I was nicer about it than Tina. Tina's in the same grade with Stacy, and honestly, I couldn't even tell if she'd heard Stacy was missing, that's how unconcerned she was. It wasn't until I saw her out back practicing her cheers that I knew she'd heard the news. Tina's been trying to get on the cheerleading squad forever, but she's convinced Stacy's been blackballing her out of spite. With Stacy gone, Tina must've figured that spot on the squad was hers. But I'll give it to you straight: I've seen Tina cheer. It isn't spite. Tina just sucks, that's all. But like I can say that, right? I like my head. I don't want it bitten off.

Mom and Dad, on the other hand, were pretty freaked out about Stacy. When I got home from school the next day, the phone was ringing. It was Mom. Then, two seconds later, Dad called. They did the same alternating phone call routine every ten minutes for the next four hours, just to make sure we hadn't been kidnapped or murdered for our snackie cakes. At one point nature called, and for obvious reasons, it took me a little longer to get to the phone. You should've heard Mom's voice. She was so shrill, she sounded like Minnie Mouse.

It was hard for me to get all worked up, though. I mean, sure, Stacy was missing and all, but it wasn't like I was looking over my shoulder every five minutes. If I wigged out over every supposed threat or rumor that went around this town, I'd be bouncing off the walls. Which of course my parents do.

Last summer, it was the gang of Jamaican drug dealers that we had to watch out for. Not that anybody ever saw a Jamaican drug dealer. That Reynolds kid with the blond dreadlocks was the closest I ever saw, but he's lived here his whole life and doesn't seem to do much except play the Galaga game down at the Happy Mart. And then the summer before that, there was a rumor that Michael Jackson was going to give a concert at the school auditorium. Which probably doesn't rank as a threat exactly, but heck, I was freaked out.

None of them turned out to be true, of course, but the whole town was in an uproar anyway. And the *Daily Squealer* tabloid newspaper covered them like they were true. I don't know of another town this small that's able to sustain its own tabloid newspaper, but hey, what can I say. There's really not a lot going on around here, so people take whatever excitement they can get.

It was like that all week—the parents and grown-ups

went out hunting for Stacy while us kids were penned up inside like little fuzzy bunnies. It really ticked me off. Partly because I figured us fuzzy bunnies were the ones who actually had a clue where to look for her, but mostly it was because that meant I was stuck in the house with Tina and our dog, Mr. Boots. All week long. For hours. You have no idea.

Mr. Boots is a great dog, don't get me wrong. We've bonded. We have a very cordial relationship. But I'm powerless to save him from the whims of Tina, and I think he holds that against me.

Mr. Boots is this weird-looking, runty Chihuahua with ears way too big for his head, and he has the misfortune of being the perfect size to fit into all of Tina's old doll clothes. It's really sad. I'll put it this way—when Mom and Dad summoned us for an official "talk" Monday night, Mr. Boots came wearing a charming blue gingham dress with lace sleeves and matching bonnet.

"Girls," Dad started, clearing his throat and trying not to stare at Mr. Boots, "it's like this."

"PTA!" Mom shrieked. Tina and I exchanged looks. Mom was definitely on the edge. I almost wanted to check the freezer in the basement for Filet o' Stacy, that's how weird she was acting.

Mom must've known she was cracking, because her face got bright red and she licked her lips nervously.

"It's a PTA meeting, kids," she said, obviously controlling herself.

Dad cleared his throat again, like he had some kind of condition. "Just a PTA meeting to talk about school issues."

"Emergency meeting," Mom squeaked.

Dad shot her a nasty look. "Nothing to worry about. Just school issues."

"What, like dress code?" I said. I couldn't help myself. I mean, like we couldn't guess what it was really about.

Dad's face turned a sort of dusty rose, the same color as Mom's bathroom, and the vein on his forehead bulged out.

"So I can go out with Trey then?" Tina interrupted,

glaring up from the squishy center of the couch. Tina has no patience for family meetings.

You'd think she'd just asked for permission to behead the neighbor's cat from the way they reacted. Mom sucked her breath in so fast, she almost choked on her own spit, and Dad slammed his fist down on the mantel, accidentally squashing a mini Snickers bar that I'd had designs on all day. I don't even know who'd stashed it there, but I'd been thinking finders keepers. Thanks to Dad, that mini Snickers was going to miss an important appointment with my stomach.

"You are staying right here until this gets straightened out, young lady." Dad wiped caramel and nougat off his hand.

"Think about Stacy! Tina, please!" Mom cried.

Tina narrowed her eyes and stared at Mom and Dad coldly for a couple of seconds. "Peachy."

Then she clenched her jaw for effect and inspected Mr. Boots's toenails. Mr. Boots blinked his watery eyes in terror. Poor guy. He could see what was coming.

"That's my girl," Dad beamed, patting Tina on the head. I think he got nougat in her hair. "Arlie, you mind Tina now."

"Great." I tried not to sound surly. Dad gets mad when you sound surly. Unbelievably, my Little Miss Sunshine routine fooled him.

Mom and Dad kissed us good-bye like they were leaving on a world tour and headed out the door. Tina promptly scooped Mr. Boots up and stomped upstairs.

"Don't bother me. I'm busy," she yelled as she slammed her door behind her.

Like I would. Like I enjoy playing fashion model any more than Mr. Boots does. Believe me, the days of Arlie, Tina's human doll, are far in the past. Besides, I had better things to do.

Ever since that little "missed evacuation" episode last year, when Tina's phone habit almost caused the Jacobs family to be asphyxiated by poisonous gases (courtesy of the local chemical plant), we've had two phone lines—

one for Tina's all-important social life, and one for the rest of the family to make emergency phone calls. I figured this qualified.

Carla Tate is this girl who lives in the little squatty house across from the junior/senior high. Usually I think it must be lousy, but not on emergency PTA nights. She gets the scoop before almost anybody else, so that makes her super popular. I grabbed the cordless, sat down in the squishy center of the couch, and started dialing. And dialing. And redialing.

Apparently, I wasn't the only person in the school with the idea of calling Carla. After about twenty minutes, I gave up and called Ty.

Ty answered on the first ring, so it pretty much confirmed my suspicions. "Carla, huh?" I said.

"You too?"

"Any luck?"

Ty snorted. "Yeah, right. It's worse than a radio contest."

"Tell me about it. What'd your parents go with? Mine

went with an emergency PTA meeting." Like there even are emergency PTA meetings.

"My dad said it was a meeting of PHAPT—Parents Helping Actualize Prom Traditions. He said it was pronounced 'Phat' but with a silent second *P*. I think he must've worked on that one for a while."

Ty's dad was pretty slick, I had to admit. That one was almost believable. Prom is the hugest deal around here, you have no idea. Swear to God, some girls start planning what to wear before they start junior high. There's even a front-page "Countdown to Prom" spread in the newspaper every year. So secret parental prom organizations wouldn't surprise me at all. I was still going with the Stacy theory, though.

I hung up with Ty and started dialing again. But just hitting redial can get pretty boring, so after a couple of minutes, I decided to make s'mores to help pass the time. I figured I'd alternate—s'more, dial, s'more, dial, and so on until Carla finally answered the phone.

Besides, I figured Ty would get more out of Carla

than me anyway—he can be a pretty fast talker when he wants to and usually manages to charm the pants off people. Ty's almost as big a klutz as I am, but he tried out for junior varsity basketball last year and actually made the team. Coach Miller was like, black kid, fairly tall, must be a natural. It didn't ever seem to register with him that Ty (a) has no basketball ability whatsoever, and (b) never actually made a single basket. I think Ty'd still be on the team if he hadn't decided that he looked dorky in the shorts. So I decided my primary focus should be the s'mores—that way, if I never got through to Carla, it wouldn't be a wasted evening.

It's really incredible how many s'mores one person can pack away, given the right circumstances. I ran out of graham crackers, that's how bad it was. And I'd opened a new package. Thank goodness I'd had the foresight to make a special chocolate-free s'more for Mr. Boots before I started. I knew he'd need one after the torture Tina was putting him through.

Unfortunately, the lack of graham crackers didn't

stop my feeding frenzy. I had just stuffed four marsh-mallows into my mouth when Carla finally answered the phone.

"Yeah?" she said in this really cranky, irritated voice. I felt slightly offended.

"Cawwa," I started, trying to swallow way too many marshmallows at once. Did I mention they were the jumbo size?

Carla didn't even seem to notice my pronounced speech impediment. She sounded like a recording. A bored recording.

"Parents inside, no visible activity." Carla sighed. "Two cop cars, plus Sheriff Shifflett's there. The Walker's there too, just pacing around outside, beats me why. It's obviously about Stacy Sizemore. I'm guessing they found her since her parents drove in with Shifflett, but no official confirmation or details. That's it." Carla smacked down the phone before I was able to attempt another word. Like I could complain, though. Once again, my instincts were right on target. And now that I had the basic idea, I could just wait for the parents to fill in the details.

Ty hadn't gotten through yet, so I called him and gave him the scoop. Then I sank back down into the squishy center and stared up at the ceiling, trying to ignore my stomach. It was making some pretty scary s'more-related noises. I could tell neither of us was going to be happy later on.

I was still lying there when my parents got home. I felt like algae on the side of a fish tank and looked even worse, but did my loving parents even notice my distress? Not on your life. They bounced around the room like they'd been sucking helium. I'm not entirely sure they hadn't.

"Tina! Honey! Come down here!" Mom chirped up the stairs at Tina's locked door. Then she flopped down next to me, totally ruining the perfect state of immobility that my stomach and I had come to depend on.

"Whoo!" Mom sighed. "What a night!"

I tried to look at her without turning my head too much. I could tell she was really relieved about something. Mom goes wacky when she's relieved. Giddy even. "What?" I said.

"Wait for Tina, now," Dad said. "Tina!"

Tina flung the door open so hard it smacked against the wall, and then she swept down the stairs, Mr. Boots skittering behind her. She threw herself into the armchair just as Mr. Boots ducked under the bookcase. His toenails were hot pink and glittery.

"Well," Dad started.

"They found Stacy!" Mom piped up.

Dad glared at her for a second, but then he forgot to be angry. "That's right, girls. It's all over now. You're safe."

I glanced over at Tina, but she was inspecting her nails, maybe planning a glitterfest of her own later. I was glad I'd saved a treat for Mr. Boots, even though I had no idea how I was going to manage to feed it to him without spewing s'mores. Just the word "s'more" made my stomach turn over in protest. I tried not to think about it.

"So she's okay then?" I said.

"Okay?" Mom looked at me like I was crazy. "Oh no, hon. She's dead."

"Oh." I wasn't crazy about Stacy either, okay, but I wasn't thinking, *Whoo! Dead! Party time.*

Mom rolled her eyes at me like I was a moron. "I know it's sad. A heartbreaking tragedy. But she wasn't murdered, Arlie. She wasn't kidnapped. That's the point."

"Oh." It was all I could manage right then. Stacy being dead made those s'mores get awfully active down there.

Mom gave me a strangle hug. "We thought there was some crazed psycho killer out there after our girls! But you girls are safe, and that's all that we care about."

Tina looked up briefly. "So what, then? Give."

Dad waved his hand in the air nonchalantly. "Oh, you know these reckless kids. . . ."

"Sheriff Shifflett explained the whole thing. It was

16

a rock-climbing accident," Mom said. "Just as simple as that. She went out to the quarry, lost her grip, and fell."

It was like the bottom dropped out of my stomach. Even Tina forgot to be cool and detached and just gaped at Mom. It boggled the mind.

"Excuse me?" Tina finally said. "Rock climbing?"

"Tragic, isn't it? But she really should've known better. Cheerleading is one thing, but really, Stacy was just not athletic."

Mom seemed to think that settled things, because she bounced off toward the kitchen. "Now who wants a drink?"

Dad did, apparently, because he heaved himself up and hurried after her. "Don't you kids do any rock climbing, now, you hear?" he said, patting Tina on the arm as he passed. "Stay safe."

The family meeting was obviously over, but Tina and I didn't move a muscle. In my head I just kept seeing

Stacy Sizemore that last day, tottering down the sidewalk. I stared over at Tina, and the expression on her face was as blank as mine. Neither one of us said a word. We didn't have to. Because we both knew that nobody went rock climbing in high heels. Not even Stacy.

CHAPTER 2

"STACY SIZEMORE? ROCK CLIMBING?" TY GAPED at me like I'd just stolen his lunch money. "Stacy? Rock climbing? Has Sheriff Shifflett ever SEEN Stacy Sizemore?"

"Doesn't sound like it," I said, swiping at Mr. Boots's paw with a cotton ball.

They had canceled school to have a memorial service, and I was sitting on my front steps giving Mr. Boots a reverse manicure while I filled Ty in on the Stacy situation. Mr. Boots had cleverly smeared his hot pink polish during the night, and Tina said she'd rather be dead than have anyone think she was a sloppy manicurist. Hence the reverse manicure. Mr. Boots seemed to appreciate it.

Ty still couldn't let go of the rock-climbing thing.

"I mean, did she ever do any physical activity? Even cheerleading, I never saw her break a sweat."

I shook my head. "She never even took gym."

Ty's mouth dropped open. It was a huge shock, I could tell. Gym is a pretty big deal where we live. Nothing can get you labeled a loser faster than screwing up in gym. And believe me, me and Ty are loser queen and king. As if the knot on my forehead didn't say that already.

We earned our titles the day we met—Field Day, first grade. We both were sent to the nurse's office for nosebleeds, mine from when I slammed my nose into my own knee while doing some overenthusiastic sit-ups, and Ty's from when he wiped out during the shuttle run. There aren't that many kids in this town, so when you get a title, it's yours for life. Me and Ty really lucked out, though—it's hard not to bond when you've both got gauze crammed up your nostrils.

Stacy had sidestepped the whole loser issue by claiming perpetual "woman problems." Just the idea freaked Coach Miller out so much that he never asked Stacy to explain. Too bad. Going by Stacy's definition, Mr. Boots's smeared polish would qualify as a "woman problem."

Ty shook his head and poked at a big brown grasshopper, trying to get it to jump. The grasshopper was not amused. It refused to budge, giving Ty a nasty glare instead. Ty poked it again and frowned, making his forehead go all wrinkly. At least, I think it was his forehead. A couple of months ago somebody told Ty he looked like Michael Jordan, so he shaved his head to complete the picture. Ever since, it's been hard to tell where the scalp ends and the forehead begins.

"It's not like she even went to the quarry," Ty said, poking at the grasshopper again. "She went toward town."

"Sheriff Shifflett says they found her in the quarry."

I stared at Ty's grasshopper nervously. I'm not super crazy about bugs, and that grasshopper was starting to look seriously pissed off.

"But that's just it, Arlie. I know she went toward town."

I gave him a look. I thought the whole thing was weird too, and I didn't for one minute believe that Stacy Sizemore had gone rock climbing. But come on, they found her where they found her. There's no changing that. But Ty seemed determined to.

"Listen." Ty abandoned the grasshopper for a minute. "Let's say she was going to the quarry. She was going rock climbing in her miniskirt and heels. Let's just say that's right. But to get to the quarry, she would've had to make a huge U-turn right in front of your house. And she didn't—she went straight."

"I didn't see her go straight," I said, shaking my head sulkily. I don't know why I was being so stubborn. I mean, he did have a point. Last time Stacy tried to make a U-turn, she took out Mom's entire flower bed and killed Tootie the plastic garden duck's brother, Topper.

"You were rolling on the sidewalk acting like your head had just come off." Ty glared at me and poked the grasshopper again. It raised its front leg like it wanted to smack Ty silly. I didn't blame it. I hoped the grasshopper would at least spit on him. Ty didn't seem to feel suitably guilty about my head wound.

Before I could remind Ty that his clunky size ten was the reason I'd been on the sidewalk in the first place, the screen door slammed open and Tina stomped out in her prom dress. She'd been practicing for prom all week, and today she had her hair all up in this funny upsweep. Half of it looked like it was on the verge of falling out, though, so maybe "upsweep" is the wrong word. Lucky for her, the prom was still a couple of weeks away. Maybe by then she would master the look—unless falling out was the look. I don't read enough fashion magazines to keep up.

"Mom says you're running late, Arlie." Tina pulled her dress up by the spaghetti straps and glared at me.

Real elegant. I hope she does that at the prom. "Get a move on."

I glanced down at Mr. Boots's half-pink toenails. "Just a couple of feet left, Tina. I'm almost done."

Tina rolled her eyes like she'd never seen a bigger idiot. "The dentist, remember? You've got an appointment. Like, now?"

I gasped in horror. I'd forgotten all about it. "But—Mom said I didn't—because of Stacy," I stammered, trying to form a complete sentence. There had to be a way out.

"Stacy's old news now, Arlie. Mom doesn't care where we go anymore. Get a move on." Tina's eyes narrowed as she looked down at us. She hiked her skirts up and started toward us. Too late, I noticed her feet. She was wearing her killing shoes.

"Ty, the grassh—," I said quickly, but it was no use. In one swift motion, Tina swooped down and crunched the grasshopper under her heel.

"Hey!" Ty said, staring at the spot on the sidewalk that had been his grasshopper friend.

"You guys are disgusting." Tina curled her lip in revulsion.

Ty's mouth had dropped almost to the sidewalk and he was shaking in outrage. "You! I can't—You—," he sputtered angrily.

"It was a roach," said Tina, scraping her heel on the step.

"It was not. It was a grasshopper."

"It was a roach," Tina repeated, stomping back up the steps. "I kill roaches."

I nodded sympathetically at Ty. "She does." I chose not to mention that Tina's definition of roach includes spiders, beetles, caterpillars, dead leaves, bits of fluff, dust bunnies, and other assorted crawly things.

Ty just gaped at me. He was having a bad morning.

That's the problem with Tina—she's got the whole beauty-queen thing going on, with the blond superstar-type looks, perfect makeup, curled hair, the whole she-bang. Mom always tells me that we look alike, but I'm pretty sure it's more in that before-and-after-picture kind of way. It makes people like Ty forget that deep down, underneath that perfect exterior, Tina's a ruthless psychopath.

I would've liked to have been sympathetic. Really. But right then I had bigger issues to deal with. Dr. Mosby was waiting, and she had a filling with my name all over it.

I have to admit, though, I was feeling pretty good when I got to Dr. Mosby's office. I have perfected the art of slow-motion hurrying, and by the time I got there, I was so late I figured they'd have no choice but to reschedule.

They didn't reschedule. Debra, Dr. Mosby's super-caffeinated hygienist, was waiting for me by the door. She whisked me back to one of Dr. Mosby's dentist cubbies before I even had time to take the gum out of my mouth. And believe me, I wish I'd had the time. Dr. Mosby was not pleased when she stuck the Novocaine needle into a wad of Juicy Fruit.

"What did I tell you about gum, Tina?" Dr. Mosby frowned, watching me spit the wad into Debra's hand.

Debra seemed even less pleased than Dr. Mosby.

"Arlie," I said, trying not to look at the needle. It was way too big to fit into my mouth comfortably. Heck, even uncomfortably.

"What?" said Dr. Mosby. She sounded distracted. Just what I love, a preoccupied dentist with a superlong needle.

"I'm Arlie," I said again, but Dr. Mosby didn't seem to care. I could've said my name was Squeaky the Dancing Squirrel for all she cared. All she wanted to do was deaden my mouth so I'd shut up.

As it turned out, the needle did fit into my mouth, a couple of times even, and it didn't hurt that much. Just that one time, when the bell on the waiting room door went off mid-jab. Dr. Mosby frowned at me like it was my fault and then patted my cheek. At first I thought she was trying to be nice, but then I figured out she was just rubbing the Novocaine in.

"You just let that settle in while I finish a few things up. I'm sorry, Tina, but you were very late."

27

"Arrwwie," I corrected, but she was already out of sight.

Waiting in the dentist chair is the worst, so I tried to pass the time by getting into the music they were playing. But it's hard to get into muzak versions of Lionel Richie, you know? I was making a valiant effort and was almost getting into the whole eighties groove when I heard Debra giggle.

That got my attention right there. In case you hadn't noticed, Debra is not a giggly person. Superefficient, yes. Scarily competent and driven, yes. Friendly and bubbly, no. Not just around me, either. Not around anyone. She's not a smiley person, period. My mom has even mentioned it before, so there you go.

I craned my head around to see what on earth could have happened to Debra. I was thinking space aliens, or a tragic nitrous oxide accident. But it was nothing that simple. She was helping someone into the mechanical chair in the next cubby.

Frankly, I was baffled.

"It's not going to hurt, is it?" the new person whined. It was a male whine too. An unattractive, wimpy whine. I stifled a snicker and drooled down my front instead. What a baby.

"Of course not, it's just a cleaning. I'll be real careful, I promise," Debra said in this really saccharine voice. And we all know what saccharine can do to you.

I craned my neck around as far as humanly possible to see if I could catch a glimpse of the whiner, but there was just too much dentist stuff lying around to get a good look. The only clear shot I had was underneath the arm of some deadly dentist machine. I scrunched down, but it was still too low.

"I brought my own painkillers. Think I'll get a discount since I brought my own painkillers?"

Debra giggled again.

They were quite a couple. I couldn't decide which one of them was more annoying. I finally settled on Debra. If she kept it up, I thought I might have to throttle her.

"Isn't that smart?" Debra cooed to the moron. "I've

29

never met a man with the foresight to bring his own painkillers. But I don't think we'll need them. It's not going to hurt."

"It's not? You promise?"

"Would I lie to you?" Debra giggled.

Dr. Mosby would kill me if I got out of the mechanical chair, but I'd reached my breaking point. I had to know.

Doing a quick check for an approaching dentist, I pushed one of the little buttons on the side of the mechanical chair. Leaning back was the only way I was going to get low enough for a good look, and it's not like the chairs are that complicated. At first I messed it up and made the chair sit up straighter, but I fixed that fairly quickly, and pretty soon the chair had gone back enough that I was lying flat. I was afraid Debra was going to hear, but with all the giggling and sighing and stuff that was going on over there, I think I could've given a root canal to an elephant without anyone noticing.

At first I could only see the moron's hat on the floor next to the chair. But it was enough. I couldn't believe it. I jabbed at the button again, trying to get the chair to lower faster. The headrest was practically touching the floor by the time I could see his face. Even upside down, there was no doubt who the big baby was. It was Sheriff Shifflett.

Well, duh. Honestly, I should've known that one right off the bat. There's only one person in this town who can immediately reduce 90 percent of the female population to drooling, blithering idiots, and that's Sheriff Shifflett. I don't know if it's the cologne, the dark wavy hair, or the way he leers at you, but if someone could bottle it, they'd make a million. Personally, I'm just glad I'm immune.

"I can't believe the way you handled that whole Stacy thing, Buck. You sure were brave. You'll be re-elected in November for sure." Debra sighed. She was doing something dentisty on the other side of Sheriff Shifflett's carefully styled hair, so I couldn't see the look on her face. But I'll bet it was sickening.

"Gal slipped rock climbing. Wasn't much to be brave about." Sheriff Shifflett's ears had turned bright pink.

"That's not the way I heard it," Debra simpered, snapping her latex gloves. Sheriff Shifflett and I both winced.

"Well . . ." Sheriff Shifflett grinned slightly and licked his lips. "Just between you and me, hon . . ." He looked around, hesitating. For a second, I was afraid he was going to notice my feet sticking way up over the top of the cubby wall, but he didn't seem to. I think they felt higher than they were because my head was so low. I tried pushing the button so I would sit back up, but nothing happened. I tried again—nothing. This was so not good. I was in for a world of pain when Dr. Mosby came back. I tried to listen and get into the cool feeling of lying upside down, but it's hard to relax when your Mosby radar is on high alert.

"Just between you and me, you're right on the money. Wasn't all quite the way we made out."

"You mean she didn't fall rock climbing?" Debra gave a fakey little gasp. Please. I was so unconvinced.

Sheriff Shifflett lapped it up. "Hell, Debbie, she wasn't even near that quarry. Up near Lake Heather, that's where we found her car. Didn't want to start a panic, though. You know those kids're all up at the lake these days."

They're holding the prom up at Lake Heather this year, and it's all anybody's talking about, or it was before the whole Stacy thing. The theme was supposed to be a secret, but everybody knows it's some kind of "Romance on the Lake" or "Waves of Love" theme. They're building a big platform for dancing right over the lake. Stupid, really, but if you help build the platform you get extra credit in Spanish. Pretty good deal. Stacy had worked it out. She was prom chairperson.

The blood was really starting to rush to my head, and I was beginning to think that it wasn't a good idea to get Novocained and then stand practically on your head. But this was too good to miss. I told myself the Novocaine would be good for the lump on my forehead and tried to focus on what Sheriff Shifflett was saying.

Debra nodded solemnly. "So that's where they found her, then? The lake?"

Sheriff Shifflett glanced around again and lowered his voice conspiratorially. "That's just it," he said. "Didn't find her whole body. Just found pieces."

I wanted to barf. Maybe it was the Novocaine, maybe it was the way the sheriff seemed to be a little too excited about chunks of Stacy down at Lake Heather. I don't know. But I didn't want to hear any more. I tried again to push the button to sit back up, but while I'd been eavesdropping on the sheriff, gravity had been doing its thing. I'd slid so far down the chair that my head was half on the floor, and there was no way I could wiggle back up far enough to reach the little button anymore. Even if I could, what was I going to do, start singing along with Lionel? Face it, I was stuck.

"Pieces? That's disgusting."

Thank you, Debra. It needed saying.

"Earlobe and left foot, if I recall. We identified her by the pink pump."

My face felt like it was about to explode, it had so much blood in it. I tried to swivel my head around to locate a spit bowl, just in case, you know? But Dr. Mosby's gotten all progressive and taken them out, so I didn't even have a safety net. Like I could've reached it anyway. There was only one option left. Slide off the end of the chair, stand up, and hope nobody noticed.

"Now don't you breathe a word of this, Debbie, you hear? Principal Smoody down at the school'd have my hide if he knew I'd let this get out. We're keeping this hush-hush till after prom. Got it?"

"But isn't it dangerous?" Debra forgot to coo and bat her eyes. "What about the kids? I mean, a killer's on the loose."

Sheriff Shifflett chuckled. "Now don't you go getting all worked up, hon. I know what I'm doing. There's nothing up there that won't keep till after prom, trust me."

Debra didn't seem entirely convinced.

Sheriff Shifflett smiled smarmily and patted her latexed hand. "Nothing's going to bother those kids, 'cept for a couple of mosquitoes, maybe. I promise, won't touch a hair on their heads. No cause to start a panic. Besides, we can't go spoiling prom. It's a tradition."

Debra melted. Even she wasn't one to go against tradition. "I won't breathe a word. I wouldn't dream of it," she murmured. If Dr. Mosby didn't come back soon, I was going to be seriously ill. I took a deep breath. Sliding plan, commence.

And then, as if in answer to my prayers, Dr. Mosby came back from wherever dentists go. She stopped behind Sheriff Shifflett's head, and even upside down, I could tell she did not look happy.

"Having a nice talk?" She didn't sound happy either.

"We were just—," Debra stammered, pulling her paper mask back on.

"Doc, is it going to hurt?" Sheriff Shifflett cut in. "I was asking Debbie here if it was going to hurt."

"That what you were asking?" Dr. Mosby smiled and thought a moment. "Yes, Buck. Yes, it is."

One point for Dr. Mosby. Sheriff Shifflett gave a

small whimper as she glided back into my cubby and stopped short.

"Tina! What have you done?" Dr. Mosby gasped.

I'll admit, I must've looked pretty bad, crunched on the floor like that and all. Dr. Mosby hurried over to the chair and pressed the up button. I clutched the edges of the chair groggily as it started moving to a more level position. Did I mention how much I love Dr. Mosby?

Sheriff Shifflett cleared his throat anxiously in the other cubby.

"Somebody back there, Debbie?" he croaked. My head was starting to feel better. Good enough for me to attempt a malicious grin.

"Just one of the Jacobs girls. Tina, I think."

Sheriff Shifflett groaned. "Aw, hell."

CHAPTER 3

HERE'S A TIP. IF YOU'VE JUST BEEN MAULED BY a Novocaine-happy dentist, don't expect to be able to run home and communicate vital murder-related information with ease. It's not going to happen. Trust me.

"Ish wassn da warry! Ish Wake Edder!" I screamed for what felt like the millionth time. Ty and Mr. Boots were huddled together on the couch, staring at me like I'd just escaped from the insane asylum. I didn't blame them for being scared. I was starting to scare myself.

I'd been trying to tell Ty what Sheriff

Shifflett had said ever since I got home, but all I'd managed to do was slobber all down my front and work myself into near hysterics. A piece of paper and a pencil would've solved the problem in a second, but of course, hysterical droolers aren't known for their sensible thinking.

"Wake Edder! Wake Edder!" I spit at them. Literally, I'm afraid. I couldn't believe Ty was still as clueless as he'd been when I walked in the door. His charades skills were seriously lacking.

Ty shrugged sympathetically and passed me a Kleenex. "That's great, Arlie. Really. But you're drooling again."

I mopped up the slobber that was dribbling down my chin and threw myself into Dad's armchair in defeat. My surprise movement startled Mr. Boots so badly that he wedged himself in between two of the sofa cushions. All you could see was a set of quivering nostrils and a bit of pink chiffon. I sighed miserably. We were a pathetic bunch.

"Wake Hedder," I whimpered, fiddling with my lip. Did I mention how much I hate Dr. Mosby?

Ty rubbed his shiny head and frowned. "Wake Heather?"

I nodded so hard that my head almost came off.

"Something about Lake Heather?"

I nodded again, almost giving myself a concussion against the back of the chair. Mr. Boots's quivering nostrils disappeared farther into the sofa, replaced by scary sucking noises instead.

It took awhile for Ty to piece together the whole story, and I admit, I left out some of the more embarrassing chair-related details. But it was worth it. Ty was totally blown away.

"Cool!" Ty jumped off of the couch and landed in his most frightening kung fu pose. The sucking sounds from Mr. Boots's end of the couch got more panicked. "What are you waiting for? Let's go down there and kick some butt!"

I stopped fiddling with my lip long enough to gape at Ty. I had thought he'd understood the whole killer-on-the-loose aspect of the story. But apparently not.

"Are you crazy? Hello, there's a killer there," I said, resuming lip fiddling. My mouth was a lot better now— it just had that weird tingly feeling left.

"Awww, come on, Arlie," Ty pleaded, dropping the whole kung fu pose. "We're never going to find out anything sitting around your living room. Don't you want to find out what happened to Stacy? Don't you want to look for clues?"

In a word, no. Sure, I was curious. But I have a pretty healthy self-preservation streak too, and honestly, as much as I like to pretend my hands are lethal weapons, the truth is my kung fu moves really suck. I told Ty as much.

"We'd get creamed. Really."

Ty shrugged and rolled his eyes at me. "So we take the pooch for protection. No problem."

He fished around in between the cushions and pulled Mr. Boots out by a hind leg. Mr. Boots lay on the sofa without moving, blinking at us and gasping for air. I swear, someday that dog is going to kill himself.

41

"Mr. Boots? Protection?" Ty had to be joking. Mr. Boots's little pink chiffon dress was all hiked up in the back, and his big bat ears were trembling. Protection was a stretch.

Ty rolled his eyes at me. "Arlie, think about it. This is a real honest-to-God mystery, and we've got information nobody else has! We could totally solve it ourselves, and when we do, we'll be heroes! We will rule the school when we start high school next year. Aren't you sick of being at the bottom of the food chain?"

"Well, yeah." Ty had a point. Being a hero would definitely be a nice change. I wouldn't mind leaving Loserville behind in junior high. And from what I've seen on TV, detectives are pretty much the cool kids of the world.

"Well, come on then!" Ty scooped up Mr. Boots and shook him at me. "Even Mr. Boots is in. This is it for us, Arlie. Our big opportunity. We've got to take it."

I took a hard look at Mr. Boots jiggling in front of me. He wasn't going to be any protection. But he might be able to provide enough of a distraction for me and Ty to make an escape, if it should come to that. After all, most people didn't see a Chihuahua in a pink chiffon ensemble every day. And it's not like we'd really be in danger, right? I mean, the detectives always come out on top.

I nodded. "Okay. We'll do it. We'll rule the school."

"Great!" Ty yelled, doing a snazzy kung fu twirl. Not that there's generally much twirling in kung fu, but Ty makes it work. Mr. Boots almost passed out.

I grabbed the Flexi leash, fastened it to Mr. Boots's rhinestone collar, and popped him in the basket of my bike before he even had time to figure out what was going on. I tried to explain that we were just going on a fun trip, but I think he knew all along he was there as a decoy. He tried to shoot me disapproving looks all the way to Lake Heather, but the wind kept blowing in his eyes, and he just looked like he'd gotten something in his contacts.

I'll tell you, though, you've got to hand it to Stacy. I

don't see how anyone could get themselves killed up at Lake Heather without there being at least fifty witnesses. But then Stacy always was a superachiever.

It looked like half the school was up there working on that platform. Amber Vanderklander had taken over Stacy's job as prom chair and was standing on the back of a truck shouting instructions in halting Spanish while the rest of the kids milled around, looking confused. Señora Jenkins, the Spanish teacher, was standing by, nodding in approval. Dr. Bruce, the biology teacher, was off by himself filling Pyrex tubes with water and frowning sternly at kids who splashed by. It was pretty much what I expected, a disaster area. Ty and I wandered over to the edge of the lake, where Carla Tate was fiddling with a two-by-four.

"What's with Amber?" Ty asked, kicking a nail into the thick, murky water.

Carla snorted. "Señora Jenkins said that the only way anyone's getting extra credit in her class is if they actually incorporate Spanish into the platform."

"Does Amber even take Spanish?"

We all stared at Amber, megaphone in one hand, Spanish dictionary in the other.

"Does it sound like it?" Carla laughed, hefting the two-by-four onto her shoulder. "Who cares, though, right? Coach Miller'll be here in a minute to take over."

Carla tossed Ty a paper bag full of nails. "Amber should be able to tell you what needs doing." She grinned. "But you might want to wait for Coach Miller. *Adios*."

We nodded and waved to Carla as she hiked out into the lake. One thing I should mention about Lake Heather—it's really a kind of glorified drainage ditch, to tell the truth. It's more like a pond than a lake, but I guess Pond Heather didn't have the right ring to it. It's only got about two or three feet of thick, slimy water, tops. Underneath that is this deep, stinky mud that sucks you in. Pretty gross.

Lake Heather wouldn't be anybody's first choice for prom, not by a long shot. But the school refrigeration system gave out during Easter break, right before the seventh annual Mayonnaise Festival. One guess where all that mayonnaise was being stored. Trust me, Lake Heather was paradise compared to that cafeteria. Even Coach Miller wouldn't go near the place. They're hoping it airs out by September.

The platform was kind of neat, in a train-wreck kind of way, but the construction area was obviously not where the action was, so I nudged Ty on the foot to get his attention. Actually, that's what I meant to do. What I actually did was trip over one of Carla's two-by-fours and whack him in the shin as I tried to avoid falling on top of Mr. Boots. But the effect was pretty much the same, more or less.

"Over there," I said, pointing across the lake. "I bet that's where it happened, don't you think?"

"Will you kick me if I say no?" Ty grumbled, rubbing his shin. A big, ugly welt was forming just above the sock line.

"Sorry," I muttered, shoving the guilty two-by-four

into the lake. Carla saw me and shot me a dirty look. I was just making friends all over the place today.

"Forget it." Ty grinned, thumping me lightly on the forehead and ditching the nails behind a bush. "We're even now." He pulled his sock up over the welt and started around the shore to the other side. "Besides, check out how isolated it is. You're probably right."

I hurried after him, carefully avoiding other treacherous construction materials and dragging Mr. Boots along behind me like a pull toy. I didn't say anything to Mr. Boots, but at some point he had obviously sat in something disgusting. The whole butt of his dress was covered with gunk. I would've laughed, but the poor guy was having enough trouble just keeping up without me making fun of his personal appearance. His tiny feet kept getting sucked down by the muck, and with every step he sank a little lower. He was a much shorter dog now than he'd been a couple of hours ago. His little mouth was stretched wide in the terror pant, and it looked like his chin was going to start grazing the ground if I didn't act fast. Call me a softie—I scooped him up, muck and all, and turned to hurry after Ty. I'd taken only a couple of steps when a hand shot out from behind a tree and grabbed onto my arm. And I looked up into the wrinkled face of the Walker.

The Walker is pretty much a local institution—he's this creepy old man who lives on the outskirts of town and spends every single day walking from his end of town to the other end and back. People pretty much steer clear of him, mostly because he doesn't really stay in one spot for more than a couple of minutes, but also because he's known to be an occasional member of the No Pants Club, if you know what I mean. He always wears a huge, baggy gray suit and carries this big walking stick, and it doesn't take much imagination to picture him beating someone to a pulp with it. If the Walker's stopped walking and taken to hanging around the lonely side of Lake Heather, it can pretty much mean just one thing. I'm here, what, ten minutes? And sure as spit, I manage to get myself killed.

I tried to jerk myself free, but it was no use—for an

old guy, the Walker kept in pretty good shape. He leaned forward and looked into my eyes, like he was trying to see inside my brain or something. I was afraid to breathe. I think Mr. Boots had gone into a coma.

"Bad place, over there," the Walker hissed, shaking my arm with each word. "Something in those woods. It's not natural. That thing'll get you. Don't go in. You don't come out."

I'd like to say I took the opportunity to ask the Walker questions about what he was saying. You know, something like, *How interesting, Mr. Walker! What exactly might one find in yonder woods?* That kind of thing. But all that really came out was a kind of gurgly grunt.

"You hear me, girl?" He shook my arm again. "Tell them others. Stay clear, you hear me?"

I gurgled again. Out of the corner of my eye, I could see Ty bobbing ineffectually near the Walker's shoulder.

"Er. Excuse me, sir?" Ty said, sounding like one of the mice in Cinderella. "Sir?"

The Walker shot Ty a glance that I swear should've

fried Ty to a crisp, and then he dropped my arm. He stabbed his stick into the ground and started off in the direction of the platform builders.

"You listen, girl," he said, shaking a gnarled finger at me. I nodded dumbly.

Ty and I watched as the Walker made his way over to where Carla Tate was hammering.

Ty did his best to whistle, which really means he blew some spitty air out of his mouth. "Man, what was that about?"

I shrugged and rubbed my arm. I was definitely going to have a bruise. "Beats me."

"The Walker's usually way over by the Happy Mart this time of day. What's he doing here?"

"I said, beats me. Now, are we checking this out or not?"

I had been ready to call it a day and just head home, but Ty was making me cranky. Besides, I wasn't going to let some old crackpot tell me what to do.

I hurried off in the direction of the trees.

The other side of Lake Heather really wasn't that far from the platform, but for some reason the low tree limbs sucked all the construction sounds away and made it seem completely deserted. It gave me the creeps, actually.

It wasn't just the weird quiet of the place that got to me, though. The truth is, the place really reeked. I mean, it was so bad, Mr. Boots tried to hide his nose in my armpit. We're talking rank.

"See anything?" Ty caught up to me. I could tell he was nervous, the way he was wrinkling and twitching his nose like a rat.

I glanced around quickly. There wasn't much to see. No footprints, stray shoes, or chunks of Stacy to be found. Just matted mucky dead leaves covered with a disgusting brownish gray slime.

"Nope, nothing," I said. After all that about Stacy from Sheriff Shifflett, and what the Walker had said, I was expecting a scene from a horror movie or something. Not your basic woodland reekfest. It was a definite anticlimax. For a second I thought I saw something out of the corner of my eye—something wide and tall looming over in the trees, but when I looked, there was nothing there, just a slight rustling of the bushes. Squirrels or something, probably. I wasn't about to let the Walker make me paranoid. "Guess we were wrong. Want to get going?"

Ty shook his head. "We're here, right? We should check a little."

I grinned at him. "It looks like the trees puked."

Ty snorted. "Smells like it too. Let's look quick and get out of here."

We poked around in the underbrush for a couple of minutes, but honestly, we just weren't into it. It was only May, but it was already so hot that my shirt was starting to stick to my back. Add that to the crawly, slimy feeling I was getting from pawing through those nasty leaves, and the gag reflex that was kicking in from the smell, and I wanted out of there.

Besides—and I would've thought this no matter what the place smelled like—it was all wrong.

"Face it, Ty." I snickered, wiping my hands on my

jeans. "Stacy wouldn't be caught dead in a place like this."

Ty glared at me for a second like he hadn't gotten the joke, and then, with an evil grin, he scooped up a big mucky chunk of leaves and hurled it straight at my head. Most of it missed, but a slimy corner of the hunk splatted right on my ear. A little blob dripped on my shoulder. That did it. This meant war. Sad to say, war means casualties, and Mr. Boots was the first to go. I chucked him into a nearby hedge and bent over to scoop up some slimy ammunition of my own. Unfortunately, that's when Tammy Banks decided to show up.

Presented with the sight of my butt hovering in the air like that, anyone would have done what Tammy did, I suppose. I can't even swear that I wouldn't have taken advantage of the opportunity myself. But she didn't have to enjoy it so much. My butt had hardly been in the air a second before Tammy's foot planted itself and gave a firm shove. There was only one thing I could do. Naturally, I went flying face-first into the muck.

"Oh, excuse me. Did I do that?"

Even if I hadn't gotten a glimpse of bright green sneakers, I would've known that voice anywhere. Me and Tammy have had the same gym period ever since I was in second grade and she was in fourth, and I've gotten used to having that whiny voice screeching at me, usually after I've missed the volleyball or had my scooter wheels lock up in scooter crab soccer. I think she looked at me that first day and thought, *Hmm, short, scrawny kid? Perfect target.* Plus she's one of those perfect attendance kids, so she never misses an opportunity to chew me up and spit me onto the wall of the gym. She's a joy, really.

"Come on, Tammy, cut it out," Ty said, not making any move to help me up.

I wiped the slime out of my eyes just in time to see Tammy give her innocent, surprised face. "Cut what out?" She smirked down at me, tossing her curly permed hair. "Can't blame me if Arlene's a tad clumsy. Always were the klutz, weren't you, honey? A real shame, isn't it, Howdy?"

I scowled up at Tammy and her goldfish-faced boyfriend, Howdy McDowell. Howdy just smiled his usual vacant, bug-eyed smile back at me and nodded. I swear, sometimes I think Tammy took his brain out and locked it in her desk drawer, maybe floating in a jar of that horrible body spray he wears. Or maybe he loaned it out to one of the other basketball jocks and never got it back. Something must've happened to it. He sure doesn't seem to use it much.

I crawled awkwardly to my feet and stood up dripping slime, still with no help from Ty, I noticed. Tammy hooked her thumbs in her flashy gold lamé belt and giggled nastily. I was all set to fire off this really big comeback, I swear, but Tammy ruined it all by flicking a piece of dirt off my shoulder and noticing Mr. Boots.

"And who's this?" she said, poking Mr. Boots with the toe of her sneaker. Mr. Boots, ever the brave defender, responded by shrinking back into the foliage and emitting a low moan. It was not his best moment.

"Is this your prom date, Arlene?" Tammy smirked. "Or yours, Ty? Look, Howdy, I bet they made the dress themselves."

"That's Mr. Boots," I said, ever the quick wit. I think my brain must be lurking somewhere with Howdy's.

"Mr. Boots? Adorable. It's easy to see who got the looks in your family. Howdy? Willow branches, remember?" Tammy threw the words back as she stalked past me and Ty down the path deeper into the woods. Howdy trailed behind her like a larger and more masculinely dressed Mr. Boots. I felt like barfing.

"Great comeback, Arlie," Ty said with a scowl, kicking at the muck after they were gone.

"Thanks for watching my back, Ty." I scowled back, scooping up the shivering Mr. Boots. I was in a foul mood, I had slime caked in my hair, and I stank to high heaven—an appealing combo of lake funk and body spray overload, courtesy of Howdy. The day had taken a nasty turn.

We headed home in silence, and I had pretty much decided not to speak to Ty anymore after that. I think I would've stuck to my guns, too, if it hadn't been for what happened in gym the next day.

Tammy and Howdy weren't there.

CHAPTER 4

"BOY, I CAN'T BELIEVE HOWDY AND TAMMY JUST ran off like that!" Marty Bollinger said through a mouthful of yogurt.

Me and Ty had decided to try to snag spots with Marty and Amber Vanderklander the next day during second lunch. Now that the cafeteria was history, people pretty much staked out their own lunch territory. The benches in front of the school are prime real estate, and prime real estate usually belongs to Amber, so she wasn't hard to find. And luckily, she and Marty were in such gossipy moods about the whole Tammy and Howdy thing that they didn't seem to notice we weren't part of their usual group.

"Is that what happened? They ran off together?" I said, keeping an eye out for Tina. I had forgotten to make a sandwich the night before, so the bologna and Wonder Bread special I was munching on belonged to her.

"It's so romantic." Amber sighed heavily, gazing off into the distance like she hadn't even heard me. Ty was sitting next to Marty, and he said later that he thought she was just being wistful. I think she was trying to avoid looking into Marty's open mouth. I know I was.

"I think it's stupid!" Marty said with gusto. "They're too young to get married! They're going to be so embarrassed when they come slinking back here."

If they come slinking back, I almost said. I caught myself in time, but the look on Ty's face told me he was thinking the same thing.

"And she never said a word! Can you imagine? That whole time up at the lake, and she never let on once."

Amber sighed again. "And you know we tell each other everything."

I pretended that I knew. "I hope she and Howdy will be very happy," I said lamely.

"So who did they tell, anyway?" Ty asked, casually munching on a banana.

"What do you mean?" Amber blinked like she'd just noticed we were there.

"They must've told somebody, right? How do you know they ran off together?"

"Oh, Buck told us." Amber waved her hand airily. "He figured it all out."

"Buck?" I almost gagged on Tina's bologna.

Amber gave me a nasty glare. "Buck Shifflett? The sheriff? He would know." I must've forgotten that being sheriff automatically makes you omnipotent.

"Sheriff Shifflett is going to help us with the platform and everything," Marty said, scarfing down a bag of potato chips.

I pried the bread loose from the top of my mouth

with my tongue while simultaneously exchanging significant glances with Ty. Quite an accomplishment, if I do say so myself.

"You don't think it's weird that she didn't say anything, though?" I said casually. Or at least, I meant it to be casual. I think it must've come off like some kind of challenge, because Amber started shooting killer laser looks at my head.

"Of course it's weird, but that's just what people in love *do*. What, you don't think Buck Shifflett would *lie*, do you?"

That's exactly what I thought, but it's not like I could say so. "Well, maybe they didn't run off. . . . Maybe they . . ."

Amber's eyes narrowed, and she shot me such an evil look I was surprised my hair didn't catch on fire.

". . . they . . . just went on . . . vacation or something . . . ," I tapered off pathetically. I can always be counted on to wimp out at the last second. Lucky for me, Ty stepped in.

"It's just so cool, Amber, that's all," he said, offering her one of his chocolate chip cookies. "I mean, wow."

"Yeah, I know." Amber bit into a cookie viciously, spewing crumbs all over her white miniskirt. She didn't even check for chocolate stains, so you know she was pissed. "I don't know why people can't just be glad for Tammy and Howdy. But I guess some people aren't happy unless they're picking apart other people's lives."

That was meant for me, if you hadn't noticed. I did, and was going to attempt a snappy comeback, when for the second time in as many days, the moment was totally ruined.

"ARLIE!"

There's only one person I know who can scream like that, and at that moment I was finishing the last bite of her sandwich. It seemed like a good time to make my escape.

"Gotta go! See you guys later." I hopped up and grabbed my books without even looking in the direction of Tina's voice. I didn't need to see her to know I was in it up to my eyeballs.

Ty hopped up too, and we both scooted across the lawn as fast as we could. Not that there was any chance of Tina chasing us, mind you. Tina has a policy against running, period, and it would be mortifying to be seen beating the crap out of your sister over a sandwich. Besides, she might break a nail. I was safe until four o'clock, anyway.

"Man, what was that?" said Ty, leaning against the brick wall outside the wood shop.

"I know!" I gasped, plopping down onto the grass. "It's just a sandwich, for goodness' sake. You'd think I'd stolen Mr. Boots's firstborn."

Ty rolled his eyes. "About Tammy and Howdy, dork."

"Ran off together, my butt," I said. "They're toast."

"Pieces." Ty made a face.

"You think?"

Ty nodded knowingly. "They sure as heck weren't about to elope when we saw them."

"So what we have here—"

"Is someone who kills girls with distinctive footwear."

Not exactly what I was about to say, but now that he mentioned it, it was pretty much true.

"Or kids who bathe in perfume." I swear, I still had some of that body spray smell in my nose, and it was driving me crazy.

"The only question is who," Ty said.

"You know who I bet did it?" I lowered my voice to a whisper. Chances were nobody in wood shop could hear us over the power tools, but you never could tell. "I bet it was Sheriff Shifflett. Why else is he covering it all up?"

"Beats me," said Ty, squatting down next to me. "But I bet you're right. And we were right at ground zero yesterday."

I kind of wish he hadn't said that, because it gave me the creeps. Not that I have distinctive footwear or anything—grubby gray Keds are as undistinctive as you can get—and it's not like I even have perfume. But just knowing we'd been so close to a killer freaked me out.

"Sheriff Shifflett wasn't there, though. Was he?" I couldn't remember seeing him at the lake at all. Something wasn't right there. For some reason, the Walker's warnings flashed across my mind. I lowered my voice. "Do you think the Walker could be right? That there's something up there?"

Ty shook his head, like I was an irritating bug clinging to his ear. "You know the Walker—he's completely off his rocker. Nope, definitely Shifflett. Probably showed up later. Come on."

The warning bell for the end of second lunch blasted right above our heads, and I grabbed my books with a sigh. Biology was next, and I hadn't even studied for the surprise pop quiz Dr. Bruce always had on Wednesdays.

But Ty wasn't heading toward the building.

"What the—," I said, hurrying to catch up with him.

"I heard Dr. Bruce isn't even having class today— he's just sending everybody to the library for a research period." Ty raised his eyebrows significantly. "And I'm pretty sure lakeside detective work qualifies as research."

I hung back. If there really was a crazed killer out there, I sure didn't want to spend the afternoon hanging out with him. Plus my nose was still recovering from our last excursion. "What, do you *want* to get killed?"

Ty grinned. "Come on, if Shifflett's there, we'll just steer clear. We'll keep an eye out for the Walker, too— could be that he's done a nosedive into the deep end, although pieces? That doesn't seem like his thing. But if it's like he said, don't you want to be the one to find out? Heroes, remember?"

He had me there. You have to be tough if you're going to rule the school. It was time for tough Arlie to make an appearance. I grinned at him. "Think anyone will notice we're gone?"

Ty shook his head. "Not a chance. Besides, it's kind of biology, right?"

Sounded good enough for me. We grabbed our bikes and headed off toward the lake as fast as we could. Fast is relative, though, when you've got to go halfway across the county on a three-speed. I tried to distract myself by counting all the RE-ELECT SHERIFF SHIFFLETT signs on the way, but I lost count. Seriously, I don't know why he bothers. The way all the women in town drool over him (and to be fair, some of the guys, too), he's got to have the election practically locked up, right? You'd think the guy would relax.

By the time we made it to the lake, my legs were burning and it was almost time for school to let out. Those smug kids with cars would be showing up to work on the platform in no time. We had to work fast.

We ditched our bikes at the foot of the path and raced up toward the lake. Ty is a real show-off when it comes to sprinting, so he had zipped around the bend before I'd even made it halfway up the path. I gritted my teeth and tried to catch up.

Coach Miller always gets on me when we're doing relay races in gym because I have this bad habit of staring at the ground when I run. It bugs the heck out of him, but it's never bothered me one bit—not until now, that is. When I rounded the bend at the scrubby bush, I barreled headfirst into Sheriff Shifflett's stomach.

I guess he must tense it up a lot at school, because I've seen him dare lots of guys to hit him, and he's never doubled up the way he did when I slammed into him. I thought for a second he was going to be sick, but he just hunched there in the dirt, re-election signs scattered all around, making squeaky gasping noises. It was really kind of awkward.

"Sorry," I said to the back of Sheriff Shifflett's head. He just made a gurgly noise. I decided to give him a minute.

"Arlene? Tyrone? What are you two doing here?"

A voice came from the edge of the water, and I turned around just in time to see someone emerging from the reeds. The ever-pleasant eau de formaldehyde tipped my nose off before my brain figured it out. I couldn't believe it. It was Dr. Bruce.

It was like Tina's sandwich had turned on me and was

trying to fight its way back out. Visions of three years of detention danced around in my head. Not only were we getting caught skipping, we were getting majorly caught by our own teacher after mugging the sheriff. Not that we took his money or anything, but still, it couldn't get any worse. I squeezed my eyes shut and braced myself for a tirade.

"What are you doing here? Aren't you supposed to be at school?" They were the words I expected to hear, but Dr. Bruce wasn't saying them. I opened one eye. It was Ty. He had his mother's best angry face on, and he folded his arms sternly as he waited for Dr. Bruce's explanation. I mean, he was practically doing the foot-tapping thing. Talk about nerve. I barely had the guts to watch him.

Dr. Bruce just blinked at Ty for a moment, his thin, weaselly face turning slightly gray. He stared down at the two petri dishes that he'd filled with the brown slime from the lake, turned from gray to pink, and coughed.

"Yes, well, I realize that," he stammered. "You're

right. I should be at school. But it's somewhat official, actually. . . ."

You could've knocked me over with a feather. I couldn't believe Ty was actually guilting Dr. Bruce into forgetting that we were skipping school. I never would've tried it. And even if I had, it never would have worked.

"Official?" I chimed in. I figured we should just keep him talking until we could make a clean break for it.

I hit the right button. Dr. Bruce looked up at us, his eyes suddenly bright. "It's fascinating work, really. If Sheriff Shifflett doesn't have any objections, it's this—"

Sheriff Shifflett gave a horrible noise like a cat hawking up a turtle, and stood up, his face blotchy and red. "You kids here for the platform?"

Ty glanced at me quickly. "Yeah, that's right. We've got study hall last period, so we got out early."

"Then get your butts over there. No call for you to be on this side of the lake. Now get!" Sheriff Shifflett growled.

He didn't need to tell us twice. We hustled back down toward the path as fast as we could without actually breaking into a run. But it still wasn't fast enough. Just before I got to the scrubby bush, Sheriff Shifflett yelled after me.

"You there," he barked. I stopped dead in my tracks and turned around. I should've known I wasn't going to get away with punching the sheriff in the stomach. It just didn't happen.

"Yeah?" I tried to be casual.

"You're one of those Jacobs girls, aren't you?" Sheriff Shifflett hitched his thumbs in his belt and strolled down the path toward me.

"Yeah." I was so dead.

"You Tina?" the sheriff growled, watching me closely.

"Arlie," I said, feeling a tiny trickle of relief. "I'm Arlie."

"Oh." Sheriff Shifflett seemed a little thrown. "Well, don't you listen to anything Tina might say, you hear? She's nothing but a little gossip, telling stories. No offense, now," he added, like'd he just remembered she was my sister and all.

I nodded and hurried off down the path. If Tina ever heard about this one, I wouldn't be able to go home for a week. Heck, maybe two. She'd probably end up giving Mr. Boots a curly perm to vent her frustration. I'd just have to make sure she didn't know.

I ran down to the platform, where Ty was carefully arranging two boards to look like he was actually work-ing. I grabbed a hammer and crunched dead leaves in the dirt until the carloads of kids from school started getting there. Sheriff Shifflett stood on the opposite side of the lake the whole time, never taking his eyes off of us. Not even when he helped Dr. Bruce load some stuff into his patrol car. Not even when the Walker showed up and Sheriff Shifflett chased him off down the road.

I was sure relieved when Amber and the other groupies finally showed up. With all the fawning they were doing, Sheriff Shifflett would've had to be blind not to be distracted. And blindness might not even have helped—I swear I saw Amber flip her hair into his face a couple of times.

It was pretty easy to slip away during all the posing and preening. But even after I got home that night, I swear, I could still feel his eyes boring into the back of my head.

CHAPTER 5

"SO," SAID TY, DOODLING ON HIS NOTEBOOK. "Who do you think it was, anyway?"

We were sitting on the floor in the main hallway before school, watching for girls with distinctive footwear. We figured it would be helpful to identify potential victims.

We'd tried identifying the heavy perfume users, but we had to abandon that plan after we got too close to Mrs. Marshall in the library and pretty much lost the ability to smell. I don't know what perfume she was wearing, but my pizza tasted like it at lunch, it was that strong.

"Who what was? The killer? I already said."

"That slime Dr. Bruce was collecting." Ty chewed thoughtfully on his pen. "Think it was Howdy or Tammy?"

"Shut up!" I squeaked, in this strangled voice. It was a pretty good imitation of Mom panicking, or of Minnie Mouse on helium, take your pick. It was also embarrassing—Amber Vanderklander and her pack stopped talking to stare at me. I scowled at them and smacked Ty on the arm, almost making him write on himself. "That's for being gross."

"Hey!" Ty wiped at his face and glared at me. "Excuse me for being realistic. That slime's got to be connected. I never noticed it before this week."

"Sure. And Dr. Bruce is up there collecting Howdy samples for biology this afternoon. Makes perfect sense, Ty." I cracked my gum at him in my most annoying way.

Ty slammed his notebook shut. "Fine. Pieces, sure, but slime? How could I be so repulsive?"

This slime thing was actually our second fight of

the morning. We'd already gotten into a near shouting match over whether Rosalie Porter's purple jelly shoes were more distinctive than Donna Cavillari's three-inch yellow platforms. I maintain they are not, but we won't get into that again.

The pathetic thing is, me and Ty weren't even that mad at each other. Not really. It was something else. It was the assembly.

Usually, when we have a school assembly, it's a really big deal for weeks. They don't have that many, especially for both the junior and senior high students together, so they really hype them up. They don't just spring them on us. Not until today.

Principal Smoody was pacing the hallways when the first bus drove up, trying to stretch his face into something resembling a smile and rubbing his bulgy stomach the way he does when he's nervous. Ty calls it his pregnancy stance, and usually it's enough to make milk come out of your nose, but today it stopped us cold. Because standing right next to him was Sheriff Shifflett.

Now, I don't think skipping school is a prosecutable offense, but you never know, right? And assault definitely is, and my little run-in with Shifflett was still hanging over my head. I couldn't figure out why else Sheriff Shifflett would be hanging out with Principal Smoody. So we weren't taking any chances. I'm not cut out for jail, and you can't arrest someone you can't find.

Me and Ty had immediately ducked around a corner out of sight, and I grabbed the first arm I could. The arm wasn't too pleased to be grabbed, but its owner, Mitzi Chang, filled us in on the details. Apparently, Sheriff Shifflett was giving a surprise assembly later that afternoon. At least, that was the official story, but come on. My heart fell on the floor and slid under the lockers when I heard that. We were so dead.

We went ahead with our distinctive footwear plan, but neither one of us was really into it. I know of one occasion in particular where I ignored a flash of potentially distinctive red footwear. So it was almost a relief when the warning bell rang and we could stop arguing about shoes and slime.

Ty jumped up without saying a word. I hadn't meant to smack him that hard, and I meant to say so, but by the time I'd gotten my stuff together, he was long gone and I had to run to get to Spanish class. Of course I was late, and Señora Jenkins totally reamed me out. Luckily it was all in Spanish, so I have no clue what she was talking about.

I thought for sure I would run into Ty again before the assembly so we could work out some kind of defense in case we were headed for the big house, but before I knew it, Coach Miller was herding us all into the auditorium.

"Oohhhh, look. It's him," Donna Cavillari said with a sigh.

I didn't need to look to know who she was talking about, but of course I did anyway. Sheriff Shifflett was standing onstage, scanning the crowds of kids as they came in. I say standing, but posing would probably be more accurate, because he was doing that puffed-chest tough-guy stance. I felt like gagging. Instead, I hunched my shoulders and tried to hide behind Donna's ponytail.

Principal Smoody lumbered onto the stage and held up his stubby hands for quiet just as I slipped into my seat.

"Kids, please," he whimpered. "Buck Shifflett, our sheriff and school board member, has taken time out of his busy schedule today to speak to you on"—he gulped and looked sideways at Sheriff Shifflett—"good citizenship and crossing the street safely. Kids? Listen now, Sheriff Shifflett has—"

Sheriff Shifflett muscled him aside and took control of the microphone. "Now, y'all listen up," he barked. "I'm here to talk to you about being good, God-fearing citizens who know how to move from Point A, the curb on one side of the street, to Point B, the curb on the opposite side. Now let's get down to business."

He put a big poster-board sign on a stand and smacked it with a pointer. I didn't buy it for a second. I mean, come on, this is the junior/senior high. I think we've pretty much figured out how to cross the street. And if we haven't, some poster-board display with stick-figure people and stick-figure cars isn't going to help us now.

"Okay now, first things first. When you want to cross the street, you got to follow the rules. Look to your left, and if the way is clear, look to your right. You kids listening? I'm only going to say this once. You get killed by a car because you weren't listening, don't come crying to me." Sheriff Shifflett waved the pointer vaguely in the general area of the poster-board display, but he wasn't even looking at it. His beady eyes were busy scanning the seats instead.

Something clicked. If I'd been Mr. Boots, my ears would've been standing straight up. Once again, my instincts had been right on target. The sheriff didn't care about the assembly. He was looking for someone. Me.

Even if he hadn't been so obvious about it, that "don't come crying to me" line would've been a huge tip-off. Pretty much everybody in town knows that the line after

"I'm only going to say this once" is "Don't look, and there are consequences." That's Sheriff Shifflett's favorite part of the speech. I've heard him say it a million times, and I generally try to stay away from the guy. It's what he always says right before he gets geared up to tell five or six of the most disgusting "I thought the street was clear" stories that he can think up. But today he completely skipped that part.

Principal Smoody must've noticed too, because he was rubbing that belly of his like crazy.

"Sheriff Shifflett?" he said, edging nervously toward the microphone. "Would you care to elaborate?"

It was like the sheriff hadn't even heard him. An evil grin was spreading across his face as he stared straight at someone on the other side of the auditorium. He'd found whoever he was looking for. And unless he was looking in the wrong place, it wasn't me.

"What?" Sheriff Shifflett didn't even turn his head.

"About the consequences of not looking?" Principal Smoody chuckled. "Any stories, perhaps?"

Sheriff Shifflett smacked the pointer down so hard it looked like he might've bruised his hand. "I've got a story for you all right."

He grabbed the microphone off the stand and sauntered up to the edge of the stage, like he was a rock star bringing it down for a minute. "It's something more dangerous than walking in front of a car. That's right, kids." He shot a meaningful look toward his victim on the other side of the auditorium. "It's gossip. Sticking your nose in where it don't belong."

The way he said it, it was like he expected us to gasp in horror or something, but of course nobody did. There are lots of things worse than gossip, but like anybody was going to have the guts to break the news to Buck Shifflett. I nodded along with everybody else and leaned back in my seat to try to figure out who he was looking at. It was starting to drive me crazy, and not in a good way.

Principal Smoody didn't seem pleased with the course the assembly was taking. "Gossip?" he murmured. "Oh, yes. Bad. But back to street crossing . . ."

Sheriff Shifflett brushed the principal aside like he was an ant about to contaminate the last cupcake.

"You there," he said, pointing to the person on the other side of the auditorium. "Stand up."

A ripple of excited whispers echoed through the auditorium. I closed my eyes and tried not to look. I knew who it had to be. With that shaved head, Ty was bound to be noticeable. I forced my eyes open, but what I saw made my heart come lurching out from under the lockers and slam back into my chest. It wasn't Ty. It was Tina.

Tina wasn't overly pleased to be singled out, and she wasn't making much of an effort to hide it either. Unlike Amber and the other groupies, Tina is basically immune to the allure of Sheriff Shifflett, so going up onstage with him wasn't a huge thrill. Donna was the one I felt bad for, though. She looked jealous enough to spit green.

"Come on up here, sweetie," Sheriff Shifflett said, oozing what I think was supposed to be charm. Tina trudged up the aisle, stepping on loose pocketbooks and feet as she went. I could tell that she was not amused. Lucky for the sheriff, she'd left the killing shoes at home.

Sheriff Shifflett put his arm around Tina as she climbed up onto the stage. Donna made a noise dangerously close to a lovesick sob, but I gave her the benefit of the doubt and decided she'd choked on her gum. It was easier on my stomach.

"Now, honey," Sheriff Shifflett said, giving Tina a squeeze. "I'm here to tell you, gossip is a horrible thing, isn't that right?"

He moved the microphone in front of Tina's mouth, but she just gave it the hairy eyeball and didn't say a word. Sheriff Shifflett didn't seem to notice, though. He was on a roll.

"Now I know what you're all saying around here. About those kids, Tammy and Howdy, and that other gal, the one with the shoes. And it's all a pack of lies, that's all it is. And I don't want to hear anyone saying different, you got me?"

Sheriff Shifflett poked the microphone back into her face and gave her shoulder another squeeze, but Tina still didn't pick up her cue. "You got me, honey? I don't want to hear you spreading any rumors, okay?"

I slunk down farther in my seat. It was like I'd just gotten hit with the biggest spitball ever made. Sheriff Shifflett was letting Tina have it over what he thought she'd heard in the dentist's office. Only Tina didn't have one clue what he was talking about.

Tina came out of her zombielike trance and stared at the sheriff for a minute. Then, squinting against the overhead lights, she started to scan the audience. Trust Tina to be sharp enough to put two and two together. Even if she didn't know what the sheriff was talking about, she knew who to blame it on. I was toast.

Lucky for me, Marty Bollinger picked that moment to pipe up from the second row. "Sheriff?" he said, his voice wavering. "If it's all a pack of lies, then what happened?"

"What?" Sheriff Shifflett glared at Marty, his nostrils flaring in irritation.

"Tammy and Howdy? It's not true? They didn't run off together?" Marty's voice cracked.

"Course they ran off together, that's what I've been saying, isn't it? Wasn't no blood, was there?" Sheriff Shifflett rolled his eyes and started talking really slow. "They ran off, and don't listen to anyone who tells you different."

"But nobody told me different." Marty was practically whispering. "Blood?"

"You listen to Sheriff Shifflett, son. Don't go listening to anybody else." Shifflett was squeezing Tina's arm so hard his fingers looked like those fat Lit'l Smokies sausage links.

Marty looked so confused his head was in serious danger of blowing up. "But nobody else—but what about—but what blood—they—," he stammered.

Sheriff Shifflett narrowed his eyes and finally stopped squeezing Tina. "What's your game here, boy? You trying to make trouble? What's your name, son?"

Poor Marty looked like an ant caught under a

magnifying glass. I swear, I could almost see the smoke rising off his back. But lucky for him, Principal Smoody decided enough was enough.

"That was very inspirational, Sheriff. . . ." He coughed softly.

"What, we out of time?"

Principal Smoody rubbed his stomach so hard I thought he was going to start a fire himself. "That's right," he lied. "All out of time. Kids, let's give the sheriff a big hand."

Shifflett nodded and smiled. "And remember, kids, tell your folks, re-elect Sheriff Shifflett!"

Tina jerked away from the sheriff and stomped off-stage. Apparently, I hadn't slunk low enough in my seat, because she made a beeline right for me.

If it hadn't been for Amber and the groupies, I would be history. But Tina hadn't taken three steps off that stage before she was mobbed. Instead of humiliating Tina, Sheriff Shifflett had managed to make her a minor celebrity.

"Can you believe he hugged you? What did he smell like?" Amber said in a shrieky whisper.

"Excuse me?" Tina stared at Amber in horror.

I didn't wait to find out what Sheriff Shifflett smelled like. I streaked out of that auditorium as fast as I could. I would've been faster, except I slammed into Tina's boyfriend, Trey, halfway up the aisle. He was hovering at the edge of the crowd of groupies, and if anyone was begging for a black storm cloud to hang out over his head, it was Trey. He'd always been the jealous type, and apparently, Sheriff Shifflett's Lit'l Smokies were the last straw. You have to be pretty dimwitted to get jealous over your girlfriend going onstage at an assembly, and Trey is nothing if not dimwitted. But heck, if that tiny brain of his was going to distract Tina while I made my escape, all the better for me. I had to find Ty.

He was leaning against the auditorium wall when I got outside. "Looks like we're onto something, huh?"

"Sure does," I gasped.

Ty shook his head. "We've been up there twice, but I

never saw any blood at all. Not even a speck. Did you?"

I thought for a second. "That's weird, huh? Pieces but no blood? How come?"

Ty shrugged. "Beats me. But if we're going to find out, we've got to get back to that lake before Shifflett does. Maybe we can get Dr. Bruce to talk."

It was like the killer was on our tail the whole time, that's how fast we pedaled up there. And even though school had been out for a while, the place was still pretty empty when we got there. Sheriff Shifflett was a pretty big draw, apparently.

We ditched our bikes in the bushes and headed over toward the other side of the lake, keeping our eyes open for any sign of blood or pieces, but we didn't see anything. Not a single speck.

"They couldn't have cleaned up this well," Ty said, staring at the ground in amazement. "It doesn't make sense!"

I shook my head. I didn't have a clue what was going on. We headed up the path, but just before we went into the silent, slimy woods, we spotted Dr. Bruce crouching near the shoreline. He was filling petri dishes with slime, just like he had before.

I cleared my throat. I had a plan. Not a great one, but it was a start. I filled Ty in on my idea, and we decided I would try it out while Ty worked out a plan B back on the path.

I pushed my way through the thick, stinky trees to where Dr. Bruce was working. "Dr. Bruce?"

He looked up and smiled absently. "Oh, hi there, Arlene."

"What are you doing?" I blinked innocently.

Okay, so the plan was pretty basic. Just straight-out asking. But sometimes you'd be surprised what you can find out.

"Collecting samples."

"For what?" For the plan to be effective, you have to be pretty blunt and act entitled. I think I was doing an admirable job.

Dr. Bruce looked worried, though. "Oh, I don't

know, Arlene. Sheriff Shifflett was pretty clear on this. I shouldn't . . ."

"Oh, I've already talked to Sheriff Shifflett. It's okay." It wasn't a lie. I'd talked to him yesterday, just not about this.

Dr. Bruce looked confused. "It is? Are you sure? Because I got the distinct impression . . ."

"I know about the pieces." There, I said it. If that didn't get him, nothing would.

Dr. Bruce's face brightened, and he looked almost cheerful. "Oh, good! You do know. Well, I'm collecting samples of the slime. We think it's the key, you know."

He held out a little dish of what looked for all the world like a huge puddle of snot. Forgive me, but it was really gross. I tried to look impressed, like it was the best snot puddle I'd ever seen.

"Wow. That's great." I made a note to myself to barf later.

"Isn't it? I believe it's a creature that's gone through changes on a molecular level. A mutation of some sort."

Dr. Bruce nodded toward the lake apologetically. "This water really is filthy, I hate to say. Extremely polluted. I think that's what caused the abnormalities."

Unfortunately, at this point my plan broke down completely. Because it's hard to ask direct and leading questions when your jaw is scraping the ground. Mutation?

I was opening and closing my mouth like a snapping turtle chewing gum when I heard Sheriff Shifflett's car peel into the lot. Actually, I couldn't see the lot where I was, but back on the path, Ty started jumping up and down and mouthing something that looked an awful lot like "werewolf" but I suspect was "sheriff," because we had to hide in the bushes to avoid Sheriff Shifflett on the way back to our bikes.

"Thanks, Dr. Bruce, that's neat. Bye!" I didn't wait for an answer. I scrambled back down the path, where we proceeded to hide in the bushes, like I said. My mind was reeling. Did he mean the Walker was right? There really was something there?

I filled Ty in while we were huddled in the bushes,

but that was it for me. I decided right then and there that I didn't give a flying fling what was going on up at Lake Heather. I wasn't going back. The whole thing had gotten too big and too weird for us to handle. Buck Shifflett could have it.

CHAPTER 6

THE GUILT SET IN ON THE WAY HOME. IT DIDN'T seem right to uncover all that stuff and then just forget about it. Not without telling somebody, at least. So I came up with a plan. Just like they say in school, right? Tell a responsible adult, and then wash your hands of the whole thing. Go about your regular life with a clear conscience. I decided to bring it up a couple of nights later at dinner. Just call me a genius, okay?

"Mom?" I said, passing the mashed potatoes to my dad for the fifth time. "I think something's going on up at the lake."

"That's nice, dear," Mom replied, spooning a third helping of peas onto Tina's plate. She didn't seem to notice that Tina was just force-feeding them to Mr. Boots under the table.

"No, Mom——," I said, but apparently I wasn't priority number one right then.

"Now, Tina," Mom interrupted, spoon poised. "I hope you have some nice activities planned for your sister tonight. I trust you kids to be good and take care of yourselves."

"Activities my butt." Tina glared at Mom, totally forgetting about the loaded spoon she was cramming into Mr. Boots's mouth. I could hear him gagging from my end of the table. "I'm going out with Trey."

"Oh, no you're not, young lady. Your mother and I are going to the club, remember?" Dad put his fork down a little harder than usual, spraying everyone with a fine spattering of gravy.

"I'm going to the movies, remember?" Tina jerked her spoon out of Mr. Boots's mouth and shoved it onto her plate. Poor Mr. Boots toppled back and made weird little mouth motions. I think he was checking to make sure he still had all his teeth.

"I talked to Dr. Bruce, see . . . ," I said to no one in particular. I don't even know why I tried, honestly, because Mom cut me off right away.

"It's the Thomasons' anniversary party!" Mom wailed, accidentally showering Mr. Boots with stray peas. It was too much for the little guy. He staggered over to the corner and hocked something green and slimy into Mom's philodendron. I pretended not to notice. Even a dog needs some privacy.

"I'm sorry, Tina, but you'll just have to change your plans. We can't miss this party. That's final." Dad was using his firm and frosty voice, which is what he uses when something's not up for discussion. It's also what he uses right before he blows up.

"I can't change my plans, Dad," Tina said in her own personal firm and frosty voice. Usually I'd have a pretty good time trying to guess who would blow their stack first. But for some reason I was feeling just as stubborn as everybody else.

"I think something's mutated," I said loudly. "At the lake there's a creature and it's mutated and it's really bad."

"Mutated?" Tina stared at me like I'd just shot peas out of my nose and done a happy dance in the middle of the mashed potatoes.

"Tina, honey? Be reasonable? We've been looking forward to this party for so long." Mom's chin was quivering.

"Fifty bucks." Dad never even stopped chewing. "Final offer."

Tina sighed and smacked her spoon back onto her plate. I think my mutation talk had thrown her off her game.

"We'll drive the kid to the movies, but she's seeing something else. No way is she coming with us."

Mom smiled in relief as Dad got out his wallet. "Well, that's all settled then. Doesn't that sound fun, Arlie?"

In a word, no. But Mom stood up and started clearing the plates before I even had a chance to argue. Tina pocketed the money Dad handed over and shot me a look that practically made my milk curdle. You'd think she'd be happy that I'd just made her some easy money, but no. I was going to be paying for this all night. Even Mr. Boots looked sorry for me.

"Mutated my butt," Tina muttered as she stomped out of the dining room. She was still muttering about it when Trey knocked on the door an hour later. If there's one thing you don't want to do, it's get in the way of Tina when she's in the middle of a power play, especially when it involves the parents. She'll never let you forget it, and she'll use whatever information she has to turn you into a burning pile of rubble. Ineffective though it was, my little mutation speech had given Tina more than enough ammo.

"Guess who's coming with us," Tina growled at Trey.

"Hi," I said, waving lamely.

Trey didn't even move. He just stood frozen on the

doorstep with a fixed smile on his face. He's still learn-ing to gauge Tina's moods, and I could tell he couldn't decide what attitude to take. He went with bummed.

"Man!" he grumbled, pushing past me. "Are you serious?"

He was doing great, but really, I couldn't help but be a little offended. We spent the next ten minutes hunt-ing for Mr. Boots, but lucky for him, Tina couldn't find him. I could've told her that he was cowering under the couch, but after that whole pea episode, I didn't have the heart to rat on the little guy.

"Maybe you should leave the dog," Trey finally said after rooting through the downstairs hamper.

"I think he's sick anyway," I volunteered.

Tina rolled her eyes. "What, you think he's mutating too?"

Trey slammed the hamper, leaving two weeks' worth of dirty clothes lying on the floor. "Mutating? Ewww, what gives?"

I don't know what Trey thought we were talking

about, but I didn't feel like filling him in.

Tina sure did, though. "Arlie thinks something down at the lake is mutating."

"What, like an animal? Like our own Loch Ness monster or something? Are you serious?" Trey howled. Again, an admirable job following Tina's lead. But it really did not bode well for a fun evening out.

I shoved a pair of Dad's underwear back into the hamper and tried to ignore him.

"Isn't that right, Arlie?" Tina smirked. "Some kind of creature. She can't stop talking about it."

Tonight was going to be a joy, I could tell. I didn't even bother coming up with a snappy comeback. I wouldn't have thought of it in time anyway.

Tina stalked out of the house and slid into the front seat of Trey's junky convertible before I'd even had a chance to close the bathroom door. By the time I got outside, Trey had flipped the front seat back and was waiting impatiently for me to climb in the back. I eyed the backseat doubtfully.

Trey rolled his eyes. "What, you think there's something mutating back there, too? Geez."

Honestly, I wouldn't have been surprised. There was so much crap in the back of that car, I didn't know how I was supposed to fit in there. I mean, it was May and I had to clear a path through snow boots, a bag of rock salt, and a couple of broken ice scrapers before I could sit down. It was ridiculous.

Tina and Trey didn't seem to notice, though. Trey hadn't even bothered to take the keys out of the car when he came inside, so he hopped in, shifted into reverse, and sped down the driveway in one smooth motion. Unfortunately, it was only smooth until we got to the foot of the driveway. It's amazing how bumpy a ride can get when you hit something.

Tina didn't even bat an eye. "Arlie, check what that was, okay?"

I climbed back out over Trey's stockpile of snow supplies and poked my head around the back of the car. My stomach dropped into my tube socks. It was Tootie.

I couldn't believe it was happening again. It was just like Topper's terrible accident a couple of months ago. I didn't think I could handle another duck tragedy so soon. We hadn't found Topper's head for a couple of weeks. The only reason we did was because Mr. Boots had screamed when he found it in the bushes.

"It's Tootie!" I called to them.

"Dammit, Trey!" Tina scowled. "How many times do I have to tell you to watch the duck!"

"Sorry, honey," Trey whined. It was, as my mom likes to say, a remarkably unattractive display.

"Move up a little and I think I can save her," I said. Tootie wasn't looking good, but she seemed to be pretty much intact. She looked more wedged than hurt.

Trey nodded and slammed on the gas, stopping just short of our garage door. Tootie lay in the driveway, her chest dented in and her legs splayed out to the side.

I brushed the tire dirt off her face and tried to make her stand up, but I could tell it would take some serious duck physical therapy before she would be able to stand upright again. I couldn't even get her to balance on her heels, and I tried a couple of times. Lucky for me, I decided to see if she could balance against the lamppost right at the same time Trey decided to back the car up again. Otherwise there would've been two of us crunched up on the driveway.

"Watch it, Arlie!" Trey yelled. "You almost made me hit you!"

"Deal with Tootie later," said Tina. "We'll be late."

Like Tina cared about being late. We'd seen both of the movies at the Cineplex twice already, and they weren't even good. I mean, Adam Sandler was in one of them. Need I say more? Last time Trey and Tina went to the movies, I don't even think they made it inside—they just hung out in the front, playing that racing game they have. Tina's got the high score.

Reluctantly I climbed into the backseat again, Tootie at my side. I figured I could try to mush her back into shape during the drive.

Almost killing Tootie didn't seem to teach Trey any

lessons, though. He streaked out of the driveway so fast, I had to hold on to a snow shovel to keep my balance. It wasn't until we'd been driving for a couple of minutes that I noticed what was going on. Trey was driving in the wrong direction.

I tapped Trey on the shoulder with Tootie's beak. "What movie are you going to, anyway?"

Tina came out of her sullen trance and glanced out the window. "What the hell are you doing, Trey?" she asked grumpily.

Trey just smirked at us. "Never mind." He seemed to think he was being really cute. I leaned against the rock salt and tried to occupy myself by pushing Tootie's chest out, but she's one hard plastic duck. Nothing was going to get that dent out, except maybe a good whack with a sledgehammer. Not that I was considering it.

Tina wasn't giving up, though. "Trey? This is not the way to the Cineplex."

Trey chuckled softly and pulled over on the side of the road. "Just thought since Arlie's so obsessed, we should check these mutations out for ourselves. You know, do something different for a change." He opened his car door and started to get out. "Anyone coming?"

I knew where we were now. Part of the highway swings right around behind the gloomy side of the lake, and that's where Trey had decided to park the car. I clutched Tootie's neck a little tighter than I should've. Good thing she's plastic and couldn't complain. "You're what?"

"Oh, please. I'd like to see the movie, *comprende*?" Tina loves to torture me, it's true, but as Trey apparently hadn't discovered, she likes to be the one setting the agenda. Even Tootie could tell that Trey had really missed the boat this time. Tina's voice had a definite note of warning in it, but Trey was too far gone to pick up on it. I wished I'd never mentioned the stupid lake.

Trey slammed the door and crunched off down the gravel shoulder toward the woods. Tina snorted in disgust and then heaved her door open. I watched her crunch off after Trey for almost a full minute before I followed. I knew they were being stupid, but it didn't seem right to let them be stupid all by themselves. I wielded Tootie like a bludgeon and trotted after them.

Trey hadn't gotten that far into the woods by the time we caught up with him, though. Apparently, I'm not the only one who gets the creeps from this section of lake, because he'd only gone a couple of feet past the tree line.

"Man, Trey, what reeks?" Tina stomped up, waving her hand in front of her face. "Is it you?"

"Thanks a lot, Tina." Trey looked hurt.

"It's the slime," I said, my voice croaking like I'd just woken up. Tina stared at me for a second and then burst out laughing.

"Check out the duck!" she howled. "What, are you going to goose somebody, Arlie? Get real."

We were within throwing distance of the lake, and the slime was thicker than I'd ever seen it before. You know that repulsive slimy sludge that you find at the bottom of your bowl of half-eaten soup when you accidentally leave it under your bed for a few weeks? (Not that I know firsthand or anything. I've just heard, okay?) It was just like someone poured their big bowl of soup slime through the trees so that it dripped down and squelched under your feet. There was a strange, stinky mist rolling in too, a million times worse than the cafeteria after the mayonnaise accident.

Tina held her nose and scowled at Trey. "Ooohh, I'm so scared. Can we go now?" She rolled her eyes in disgust.

Trey looked deflated. "You're no fun." Then, in what I think was supposed to be a big macho move, he spat into the leaves. And they splashed.

We all froze. Leaves aren't supposed to splash, no matter how much you spit on them. We all stared at that blob of spit for what seemed like hours. I was listening so hard that my ears hurt. The splashing noise came again. I almost laughed at how silly we'd been, except that if the spit wasn't splashing, it meant something else was. My hand tightened around Tootie's neck as I looked toward the water. There, in the shadows under the trees, I could see it. Something was watching us.

I'm telling you, it looked like a gummy bear. Not just your average gummy bear either, but a big one, seven feet tall at least. It was that same disgusting, transparent brownish greenish color that all deformed reject gummy bears are, and it had the same stubby little arm nubbins on the sides. The only thing it was missing was that cute gummy bear face. Instead, it was like a gummy worm had eaten the bear's face and forgotten to detach itself afterward. If I hadn't been so close to wetting myself, it would've been funny.

I blinked hard and tried to convince myself that I was having a psychotic episode or something. I had almost decided that I was imagining the whole thing when I saw Trey's face. He had turned whiter than his T-shirt and was gasping like all the oxygen had been sucked out of his lungs.

Tina, on the other hand, was unfazed. "Oh please, Trey," she groaned. "You think this is funny? Ha-ha. Can we go to the movies now?"

The thing had started gliding toward us, leaving a trail of thick slime as it went. And I couldn't help but notice that it was snaking its wormy tentacle face out in our direction.

"Movie?" Trey squeaked. "Great!" He moved his arms like he thought he was running, but his feet didn't seem to be getting the message. I didn't care about Trey's feet. My feet got the message. My feet were heading for the car.

Unfortunately, my face got all tangled up in a tree branch that knocked me over and made me drop Tootie. But my feet weren't about to let that stop me. I'm ashamed to admit that in my mad dash to save my own butt, I abandoned Tootie's little plastic one. But I noticed that no one else stopped to save her either.

Trey figured out how to work his legs when I was about halfway to the car, and Tina wasn't far behind him, stomping through the woods in that speedy, irritated way that she has. I don't know if that thing was still following us. All I know is I've never been more relieved than when I skinned my knee on that gravel shoulder. Tootie seemed to be a small price to pay.

We had just made it to the car when something came shooting out of the woods, just missing my head. It whanged right into the car door, making a huge dent and bouncing off into the road. Trey gave a little scream and hopped into the driver's seat, but I had to know what it was. I couldn't believe my eyes. It was Tootie.

I didn't know how she'd made it out, but I didn't stop to ask questions. I scooped her up and hopped into the backseat, cowering under a moldy old picnic blanket I found on the floor. Tina's car door wasn't even shut before Trey peeled out onto the road. I think this had to be their worst date ever.

"It wasn't even scary, Trey. Okay? You're so lame." Tina glared out of the window. She was acting like it was some big put-on, but Trey didn't deny it. In fact, he didn't say a word the whole ride home. Nobody did.

Tootie glared at me from the opposite side of the car. The impact had dented her chest back out, and except for being a little bowlegged, she looked almost normal. I was almost afraid to touch her, though. Not that I had wanted that thing to get her, but it was pretty freaky to have her fly at us that way. I tried to take deep breaths and not think about it.

Trey made it back to our house in record time, and I was afraid Tina was going to gripe about not going to the movies, but for some reason she didn't say anything. She just got out of the car and headed for the house. I grabbed Tootie by the beak and hurried after her. I needed a s'more.

Trey sped off as soon as our butts were out of the car. I chucked Tootie into the yard and turned to head inside, but Tina blocked my way. She grabbed the neck of my shirt and jerked me around like a cat with a dead mouse.

"Not one word," she hissed, her face inches from mine. "Not a single word."

CHAPTER 7

IN THE END, IT DIDN'T MATTER WHETHER I SAID anything or not, because Trey had a big enough mouth for all of us. The big tip-off came when I woke up Monday morning and found the yearbook staff in our front yard inspecting Tootie. There was even a photographer from the *Daily Squealer*. Your average garden duck doesn't generally attract that kind of attention. By the time I'd finished breakfast, it had gotten so bad, we had to bring her inside for her own protection. Things were getting rough out there.

Big surprise that it was all over school,

then. Except, according to the version I overheard at my locker, Trey had been this big brave hero and I hadn't even been there. It was to laugh.

Not that I was too bummed to be left out of it. Trey had thoughtfully included Tina in his version, except her role was pretty much limited to screaming and crying. Tina was so mad she spent most of the day holed up in the downstairs girls' bathroom pretending to be sick.

The only person who didn't get caught up in the excitement was Ty.

"Okay, what gives?" Ty said when he saw me out front after second lunch. He didn't even say hi or anything first. He'd been out of town all weekend, so I hadn't been able to give him the scoop yet.

"Nice to see you, too," I said.

Ty rolled his eyes and spat into the dirt. He isn't usually a big spitter, unless he's gotten a gnat in his mouth or something, so I knew he was trying to be all cool. But the edge of his mouth was twitching too, so I knew he was dying to know the scoop. He's always been a big twitcher.

"I've heard all about what Trey thinks he saw up at the lake. Give me a break." Ty leaned against the water fountain, accidentally soaking the edge of his shirt. He pretended not to notice.

"What have you heard?" This had to be good.

"That there's this big sea monster up there, like a big squid or something. Give me a break." Ty rolled his eyes again, and I have to admit, I joined him. That thing I saw was nothing like a squid.

"That's a total lie." I laughed.

"I figured it was." Ty grinned. "So what do you think he saw, a fish or something?"

"Well . . ." I hesitated. Somehow I didn't think Ty was going to take this well. "It wasn't a fish. I saw it too. It was kind of different."

"Different how?"

"Different like a gummy bear."

Ty stared at me like half of my brain had just fallen onto the sidewalk and gotten run over by a dump truck. "Like a gummy bear."

"With a big gummy tentacle for a face."

Ty didn't even blink. "Yeah, that's what I figured," he deadpanned.

I went ahead and filled him in on all the details, glossing over the way I had ditched Tootie, but Ty never said a word. His face had even stopped twitching, so you know he was freaked.

"A gummy bear?" he finally said again.

I nodded. Like I would make something like that up. "It was just like the Walker and Dr. Bruce said."

Ty crumpled up his forehead. "Are you sure you weren't imagining it?"

"I'm sure."

"Because it could've been a trash bag. Those white kitchen bags can look pretty scary sometimes." Ty nodded solemnly.

I clenched my jaw and tried not to smack him one. "It wasn't a trash bag. It was a giant gummy bear."

"Could it have been a joke? Somebody playing a game with you guys? Shifflett maybe?" he suggested.

I sighed so hard I spit on myself. "Ty, for the last time, it was not a trash bag. It was not a joke. Nobody even knew we were going up there. Heck, I didn't even know. Don't you get it? This gummy bear thing is connected to the slime."

Ty scowled at me. "That is so screwed up, Arlie! We've been up there almost every day, and we never saw any gummy monster. You think something like that could just hide?"

Of course, that's when the bell rang, so we didn't get a chance to finish the conversation until after school. By which time I had totally convinced myself that Ty was completely pigheaded, and Ty had totally convinced himself that I was unable to recognize basic household kitchen products.

"It was not a trash bag!" I screamed for the millionth time. I stormed into my house and grabbed the bag out of the trash can. "I know what this is! I can recognize this. Different brands, even!" I said, shaking the bag so hard that little bits of last night's dinner fell out. Mr. Boots took one look at the peas on the front step and yakked in the bushes. "What do I have to do to prove it?"

"I just think we would've noticed a giant gummy bear!" Ty screeched back in a voice so high it sounded like it hurt. "I want to know what's going on too, Arlie, but making things up doesn't help, okay?"

That was the last straw. "Fine, you want to see the stinkin' monster?" I yelled. "We'll find the stinkin' monster." I grabbed my bike out of the bushes, accidentally tearing out half of the bush with it.

"Great. You can watch me kung fu his butt." Ty snatched his bike up, purposefully not mangling the landscaping just to show me up. "Or we can just deposit him in the proper receptacle."

He was gone before I could say another word, which was good, because I was so mad all I would've been able to do was spit or cry. And neither one was the comeback I was going for. I picked the stray branches out of my spokes and headed off toward the lake.

We'd been fighting for most of the afternoon, so

it was getting dark by the time we made it up there. Most of the kids working on the platform had skipped out already, and the only person who saw us heading up the path wasn't even a person—it was Grumpus, the neighborhood cat. He didn't care where we were going. He just hissed at us and lunged at Ty's ankle in greeting. Lucky for us, Ty dodged just in time to avoid Grumpus's fangs, and Sheriff Shifflett was too busy flirting with Amber Vanderklander to notice us slip into the woods on the other side of the lake.

I don't know who was jumpier, me or Ty. Every leaf that brushed against my skin made me feel like bolting back to the bikes. I was beginning to think this was a really stupid idea, especially since I was just out to prove I was right. I wasn't even sure I wanted to be right. It wouldn't be so cool to be right if I was also just a finger.

When we'd gotten a couple of feet from the water, Ty hesitated. "So, we should probably do what you guys did last night, huh?"

Somehow blundering around like idiots didn't seem

like the most effective strategy, but I didn't say that. "I think we should sit tight and wait."

"Is that what you did?"

"Well, not exactly."

"Oh." Ty didn't push it; he just squatted down in the bushes bobbing casually on the balls of his feet while he scanned the woods. I carefully examined a spot under a tree, making sure there weren't any stray tentacles lying around. The only thing that looked even vaguely tentacle-like was a huge, grumpy old bullfrog lying a couple of feet away. He barely even looked alive, so I figured he wouldn't be much of a threat. After one last superparanoid look around, I settled in nervously to wait. And wait. And wait some more.

Funny thing: The longer we waited, the less scared we felt. By the time it had gotten completely dark and the echo of voices had died away, we were both feeling like raging idiots. Except Ty was also a cranky raging idiot.

"See, I told you it was nothing!" he groused, bobbing creakily to his feet. "It probably wasn't even a trash bag. It was probably just a used Kleenex caught on a branch."

As Mom likes to say, I didn't even dignify that with a response. Instead, I scrambled to my feet and tried to shake my right leg awake. "It was here, Ty. I don't care if you don't believe me."

"Well, good, 'cause I don't. Thanks to you and Tina's stupid boyfriend, the whole school thinks there's a monster up here. And do you know what that means? That means a killer's walking around free."

He stuck his thumbs in the waistband of his jeans and did a goofy imitation of Sheriff Shifflett's strut, complete with hip swagger and brain-dead expression. It would've been pretty funny if I hadn't noticed something lurking in the trees behind him. The gummy monster was back.

You've got to give Ty credit. It only took him a minute to figure out something was behind him. And when he did, I swear, I've never seen anybody move faster.

"It's not a trash bag," Ty gasped as he stared back at the thing in the bushes.

I shook my head, afraid to move. I couldn't tell if the thing had noticed us, and I sure as heck didn't want to tip it off if it hadn't. "That's the thing that got them—Stacy and Howdy and Tammy."

Ty nodded and got into his best kung fu stance.

I blinked at him. Ty could be stupid, but even he couldn't be that stupid. I couldn't believe he was planning to kung fu its gummy butt. "Ty, what the heck?"

"Well, somebody's got to do something," he whispered. "And it might as well be me."

Sure, the plan was to be heroes. But somehow Ty didn't seem to be grasping the gravity of the situation. "What are you planning to do?" I didn't even want to be within a mile radius of the thing, let alone get into a kung fu match with it.

"I'm going to give it a good chop to the throat. Then, if it's real, I'll have disabled it, and if it's fake, we can find out who it is."

It seemed like a decent plan, except for two glaring problems. One, the thing looked pretty darn real to me.

And two, the thing had no throat. It was just a blob with nubbins and a tentacle. Try kung fu-ing that. But evidently, Ty wasn't going to let a little thing like no throat stop him.

But I was. I grabbed him by the shoulders and dragged him back as far as I could into the bushes.

"Ty, no, don't you dare."

Ty scowled at me. "Arlie, cut it out. How come?"

The thing wasn't moving, which I took as a good sign. "We don't know anything about it. We don't even know how it got the others. We can't risk it."

Grumpus the cat stalked over and peed on Ty's shoe.

Ty shook his foot in disgust. "Okay, can we make Grumpus go after it? As a test?"

I looked at Grumpus doubtfully. He really was a nasty cat, but somehow I didn't feel right using him as a guinea pig. I stared through the trees at the gummy thing, trying to gauge how much damage I thought it might do. It still wasn't moving. Grumpus scratched his ear, convulsed a couple of times, and shot a hairball into a nearby bush. He looked pretty tough.

"I guess so," I said.

"Cool." Ty leaned over and scooped Grumpus up around the middle.

If I had any doubts that Grumpus could take care of himself, they were gone as soon as Ty tried to lift him off the ground. Grumpus had obviously been having a really bad day, and being picked up was the last straw. Within seconds he'd turned into a hissing, spitting whirlwind, shredding everything in sight, Ty's arm included. The next thing I knew, Grumpus was flying through the foliage and streaking down the path. I don't know if he jumped or if Ty threw him, but it didn't seem to matter. Grumpus was history. On a scientific note, he did land on his feet.

"Crap," Ty whimpered, pressing his shirt to his bloody arm. "That hurt." Remind me to nominate Ty for the understatement of the year award.

He wrapped his wounded arm up in the hem of his

shirt and stared darkly into the bushes. "Guess it's up to me to give it a shot, then. Rule the school, remember?"

If there's one thing I don't recommend, it's facing a potentially life-threatening monster with wimpy kung fu skills and a shredded arm. So when Ty crept back toward the gummy thing, almost stepping on the comatose bullfrog lying in the leaves, I knew I had to do something.

"Ty!" I hissed. "Try the frog."

Ty looked down at the frog doubtfully. I was a bit skeptical myself. I mean, he was already such a dead-looking frog, I wasn't sure how we'd know if the monster killed it. But it was better than testing things out on Ty. Ty must've come to the same conclusion, because he scooped up the bullfrog and encouraged it to jump in the direction of the gummy thing.

It may have been my imagination, but it seemed like the monster was a little closer than it had been before. But I hadn't seen it move. The hair on the back of my neck stood up. In all the fuss about kung fu-ing the thing, I'd almost forgotten that it was real. But it was. And I had the nasty feeling that it was luring us closer. I didn't like it one bit. I was this close to just ditching the frog and taking off.

It looked like the frog's hopping days were over anyway, because no matter how Ty nudged it, it refused to move. I was so intent on watching that stupid frog lying there that I almost didn't notice what else was happening.

While we'd been messing with the frog, the gummy monster had made its move, slowly snaking its tentacle closer and closer until it was in the clearing where we were standing. I almost pulled a Grumpus when I noticed it. It was only about a foot away.

"Ty!" I hissed, grabbing him by the good arm and dragging him backward.

"Oh, geez!" Ty jerked back away from the tentacle. It was at that moment, when we were tripping over ourselves trying to get the heck out of there, that the frog decided to sit up.

It took one halfhearted step toward the tentacle, and then it happened, the grossest thing I'd ever seen. At first it looked like the tentacle had barely touched the frog, but it became obvious pretty fast that it had our flippered friend in some kind of vacuum grip. The frog stuck there on the end of the gummy tentacle for a second with a confused expression on his face, wiggling his froggy feet in the air. Then, slowly, he started to change. One minute the frog was sticking to that tentacle, and the next minute he was just melting away right before our eyes. I couldn't believe it was happening. The whole thing probably took a couple of minutes, tops, and when it was over, it was like the little guy was never even there.

That was bad enough, but what I saw next made it a million times worse. On the ground where the frog had been, there was a tiny flipper.

Ty saw it too. "Arlie! The foot, it's just like—" He didn't even have to say it. "Run!" he gurgled in horror as he whirled and raced out of the woods. I was right behind him, running so fast it didn't even feel like they were my feet. I'd learned my lesson, though. I wouldn't bother that thing again.

I had just cleared the woods and was racing down the path when I stumbled and felt myself falling. A scream caught in my throat. I hadn't run fast enough. Something had me by the leg.

CHAPTER 8

"RUN, TY! KEEP RUNNING!" THE SCREAM IN MY throat burst free as I smacked into the ground. Not that Ty needed me to tell him to keep going. He never slowed down for a second. When I looked up, I could barely see the puffs of dust he'd kicked up as he raced down the path. He was ditching me worse than I'd ditched Tootie. Not that I had much room to complain.

My foot was caught in a vacuum grip all right, and no matter what I did, I couldn't get free. All I could think about was that dissolving frog. I gathered my strength and kicked hard at the thing holding on to my foot. If I only had a couple of minutes before I started to melt away, I wasn't going to spend it lazily flapping my legs. I was going to do some serious damage.

"Ow! Hey!" the thing said as my foot connected. *Ow?* Somehow that didn't sound like something a gummy blob would say, but I wasn't taking any chances. I kicked it again for good measure.

"Hey!"

Pretty limited vocabulary the thing had, but I guess I shouldn't expect much from a gummy monster. What was bothering me, though, was how hard the thing was. I thought a gummy bear would feel more rubbery.

I scooted around as much as I could and glared back at the vacuum sucker attached to my foot. When I saw what I'd kicked, I went limp with relief. Thinking you're about to dissolve takes a lot out of you. But as relieved as I was, I couldn't help but groan. I was just destined for detention. I'd kicked Dr. Bruce.

It didn't take long for me to go from relief to severe

irritation. I mean, you don't just go grabbing people's ankles while they're running. It's not nice, especially when you're a teacher.

"What's your problem?" I demanded. Although it was pretty obvious that at the moment, Dr. Bruce's big problem was a bloody nose. I must've kicked him right in the face.

"How dare you, Arlene!" Dr. Bruce glared at me and pinched a grubby handkerchief over his nose. I'd never seen a science teacher looking so ticked. At least he'd let go of my ankle.

"Sorry about your nose," I said, sitting up. "I didn't know it was you."

Dr. Bruce narrowed his eyes as he lowered the hand-kerchief. It was a little soon for that, to be honest, but I didn't say anything. He was shaking, he was so mad. "How dare you."

I was getting the sense that this was about more than a nose here. Apparently I'd screwed up some other way. Not that that was surprising. I waited for Dr. Bruce to fill me in.

"Do you have any idea the damage you've done here? Do you?" Dr. Bruce shook his bloody handkerchief at me.

"No." I tried not to stare at his swelling nose. Dr. Bruce was freaking me out.

"Hours of valuable research, ruined. Do you know how many kids have been snooping around up here because of you, young lady?"

I should've known I'd get blamed somehow. "But it wasn't me . . . ," I started, but Dr. Bruce didn't want to hear it.

"I asked you to keep quiet. You gave me your word, Arlene. Thank heavens you didn't tell them exactly where I was working, or the chance for future research would be destroyed. Is that what you wanted, Arlene?" Dr. Bruce's eyes flashed, and a thin trail of blood trickled out of his nose. "Your reckless disregard for the scientific process is appalling, young lady. I should take points off your grade."

"But I didn't tell them about the pieces," I tried again. Unsuccessfully.

"A gory scavenger hunt, that's what you've turned this into." Dr. Bruce wiped at his nose with the handkerchief again, smearing blood across his cheek.

I couldn't afford to take the rap for this one. My biology grade was low enough already. "They were looking for the gummy thing we saw, Dr. Bruce, not pieces. And I didn't tell them about it, Trey Callahan did." Just call me Whiskers. I was being a total rat.

Dr. Bruce stared at me like he was starving and my head had just turned into the world's biggest cream puff. "Gummy thing? What gummy thing?"

"The gummy monster thing that makes the slime. That's what got Howdy and Tammy, right?"

Dr. Bruce's eyes gleamed. "That's my theory, yes, but until now it's only been a theory. You actually saw the creature? Where? How large was it?" Dr. Bruce was shaking so hard it looked like he was about to blast off. I wished I'd listened to Tina and kept my big mouth shut.

"In the woods back there, by the water. But I think

it's dangerous. It dissolved a frog. It just left a foot."

"Really." Dr. Bruce nodded thoughtfully. "Thank you, Arlene. That's very helpful."

I hoped he'd remember that when he went to dock my grade. "What are you going to do about it? The monster, I mean?" I probably should've just come to him about the whole thing first, instead of getting so worked up. Dr. Bruce would take care of everything now that he knew.

Dr. Bruce smiled at me with a funny, puzzled look on his face. "Do? More research, of course."

I shook my head. "No, I mean to get rid of it. So it won't dissolve any more kids."

Dr. Bruce waved his hand in the air dismissively, just like Sheriff Shifflett always does. It gave me a cold feeling in the pit of my stomach. It must've shown on my face, because Dr. Bruce hesitated and then took me by the shoulders. "I know it's hard, Arlene. What happened to those children was unfortunate, a tragedy, really. But there are always casualties in the struggle for knowledge.

You can't focus on that aspect. We can't bring them back, so we have to look to the future instead. Think of the incredible research possibilities. Isn't it wonderful?"

"Isn't it dangerous? I mean, there are kids all over the place here," I said, the cold feeling spreading. "Shouldn't you do something first? Maybe research later?"

Dr. Bruce tapped his temple. "Study, Arlene. It will reveal all. We have to understand the creature before we can defeat it." He folded up the bloody handkerchief with a smug smile and put it into his shirt pocket. The blood on his cheek had dried and cracked when he smiled. "Now, where did you see this creature? By the water, you said?"

I nodded and pointed miserably through the trees. "Right over there. But you'd better not go there now. It was just there a minute ago."

"Really." Dr. Bruce's eyes gleamed again as he hopped to his feet. "Now don't you worry, Arlene. This will be very interesting. You'll see, you're getting worked up over nothing."

He dusted himself off and picked up his briefcase from where it was lying in the leaves. "Trust me. I'm a scientist. I know what I'm doing."

It sounded good. Except I was having a hard time forgetting that Dr. Bruce had already misplaced our class's dissection pigs four times this year. So I wasn't exactly feeling confident as he tucked his briefcase under his arm and headed off through the trees.

That's not to say I stuck around, though. Heck, I didn't even wait until he was out of sight before I scrambled to my feet and headed off down the path as fast as I could. I was going to be having nightmares until I was thirty.

My bike was lying out in the middle of the path. I'm guessing from the bent spokes that it had gotten tangled up with Ty's when he was trying to make his escape, but I wasn't complaining. It just made it easier for me to get moving myself. The coldness in the pit of my stomach had turned into a hard, tennis-ball-size knot, and I was having a hard time controlling the gag reflex.

And it wasn't because Dr. Bruce had made my shirt and ankle reek like a dissection pig either. (Even though they totally did.)

I don't know why I was in such a hurry to get home. It was way past dinnertime, and I was really going to catch it for being so late. But all I wanted to do was go up to my room and hide under the covers, read the comics, and sing camp songs. Anything to take my mind off the slimy, gummy thing eating kids in the woods. Even being punished would be a relief.

Two pairs of eyes were gleaming in the bushes as I pedaled into the driveway. It really freaked me out for a second, and I considered screaming uncontrollably, but before I even got my mouth open, Ty and Mr. Boots came barreling out through the branches. Ty came scurrying over to me, and Mr. Boots started a thorough inspection of my bike. Ty was looking almost pale, even.

"You're alive?" he gasped, looking me up and down like I might go transparent on him any second. I nodded and decided not to mention the ditching. It's not like

Ty could really help it. Put him in a panic situation and his feet just start moving. He'd done the same thing to me that time he stepped on that hornet's nest (thirteen stings for me, thank you) and the time he'd been teasing Missy Barton's poodles without realizing the gate was open (sore ankles for a week), not to mention that little motorcycle-tipping incident outside Jimmy's Lounge on Route 15 (no physical scars, but who likes being held three feet in the air by their collar? Anyone?).

I glared at him. "I'm not saying anything."

Ty nodded. "I know. Add it to the list. I suck. How'd you get away?"

I sank down onto the stoop and tried to breathe like a normal person. My insides felt all twisted wrong.

"It was Dr. Bruce," I said, a catch in my throat. "He grabbed my foot. He knows all about the monster, but he's not going to do anything." I almost started bawling right then, but Mom chose that moment to stick her head out of the kitchen window.

"Oh, good!" she chirped. "You two are back. Did you

have a nice dinner, Arlie?" Mom smiled her reminding-me-to-be-polite smile. I frowned and looked at Ty.

Ty was nodding like crazy and smiling a big fakey smile. "We had a casserole, Mrs. Jacobs. And pie." He jabbed me in the side with his elbow.

"It was really good," I said, catching on. "Thanks, Ty." At least I wouldn't be grounded.

"Glad to hear it. Don't be long, now," said Mom, ducking her head back in the window. I had about two minutes.

"We'll think of something," Ty hissed, picking up his bike. "Don't worry, they can't just leave it there. This whole thing is practically over."

I tried to believe him. But the truth was, that thing was still up there, and there wasn't anybody to stop it. This wasn't the end of anything. It was just the beginning.

CHAPTER 9

"ACTUALLY, MAYBE IT'S NOT SUCH A HUGE DEAL," Ty said the next day at lunch. I almost gagged on a corn chip, that's how shocked I was.

"Not a huge deal?" I cried, accidentally spraying Ty with chewed-up chip. "How can you say that?" Finding a big, blobby gummy monster munching on your classmates in the woods struck me as pretty high up on the hugeness scale. Granted, it isn't the kind of thing to make the covers of the teen magazines, but I think that just proves how huge it is. Ty was obviously insane. Either that or possessed. I was leaning toward possessed.

"No, listen," Ty said, discreetly wiping flecks of chip off his face. "Hear me out, okay? I think I've got this figured out."

I shoved the chips away and sat back to listen. I had no business trying to eat during this. Ty would only end up wearing whatever I put in my mouth.

"Let's hear it." I tried to sound open-minded.

"Okay." Ty leaned forward on the bench. "That thing is pretty creepy, I'll give you that. And disgusting."

"And dangerous."

"Right. Dangerous." Ty nodded. "If you get too close. But maybe it's not that bad otherwise."

I raised my eyebrows. This open-minded thing wasn't going to be easy. "And how's that?"

"Think about it, Arlie," he said. "We've been up there a lot lately, and we're still around, right?"

Like he expected me to argue. I just nodded and eyed the chips.

"And when we did see it, that thing barely moved at

all. Sure, what it did to that frog was disgusting, but it's not like it didn't have time to get away. The way I figure it, you have to be pretty slow or pretty stupid to get eaten by that thing."

He had a point. It wasn't a very animated monster, except for that tentacle. "So you're saying that Stacy and Tammy and Howdy were just stupid?"

Ty grinned. "Well, come on. How smart do you have to be to run away? I mean, it's a blob."

Two points for Ty. Still, dangerous or not, I didn't like the idea of a hungry gummy blob lurking in the woods, even if it wasn't that mobile. I shook my head and took a chip. "I don't know, Ty."

Ty shrugged and crumpled up his lunch bag. "Well, think it over. It's not like it's running around terrorizing the town. It actually seems pretty shy—it doesn't even like to come over where the people are. The only reason we even know about it is because it's not a member of the clean plate club."

He hopped up and tossed his lunch bag at the trash

can. I don't know what he was thinking, because the trash can was more than ten feet away, but Ty still looked bummed when he missed. I swear, ever since he shaved his head, he thinks he can play like Michael Jordan too.

I stared off into the distance, trying to look thoughtful as I munched on my chips. It was hard to come up with a convincing argument on an empty stomach, but I was sure there was one. I just couldn't figure out what it was yet. It didn't help that I was totally distracted by what was going on in the parking lot.

Tina was streaking past the cars, with Trey bumbling along at her heels. His first mistake was trying to keep up with that superfast walk of hers, which I know from experience is impossible. His second mistake was to try to do it while loaded down with both of their books. The whole scene was cringeworthy. He was practically begging Tina to forgive him for the stupid stuff he'd said yesterday, but it wasn't working. And it was about to get worse. Trey was so intent on watching Tina's face for a flicker of forgiveness that he didn't notice that she was heading straight for Principal Smoody's wife, Bunny.

I don't mean in the general direction of either, I mean straight for. Trey had it coming, sure, but I felt pretty bad for Bunny. You could tell just by looking at her that she wasn't her usual bouncy self today. She didn't make many appearances at school, and when she did, she usually had that happy–happy face on. But today she was wearing the I'm–about–to–freak–out face that Mom always gets when you do something little like spill soda on the new sofa cushions or something. Tina could be so cruel.

When she was just two steps away from Bunny, Tina stepped neatly to the side and swerved around her. What happened next was just like a cartoon. Trey's eyes got wide and he tried to swerve at the exact moment Bunny put on the happy face and started to walk toward the school. You could practically see the stars swirling around their heads when they hit. Bunny screamed like Trey was the world's biggest rat as her light blue pump sailed across the parking lot. Trey ended up face-first on the pavement, books scattered everywhere. Tina didn't even look back, but she was definitely smirking as she slipped into the side entrance.

Ty nodded in the direction of the parking lot carnage. "Am I wrong?" He grinned. "I mean, Trey escaped, didn't he?"

That did it. I burst out laughing. Maybe it was the stress of the past week that made me get the giggles, I don't know. But all of a sudden I figured Ty was right. It didn't seem so bad.

"Besides, Sheriff Shifflett's guarding the place pretty well, right?" I said. "It's not like anybody else is going to get eaten."

"Yeah," Ty agreed. "And I bet they get rid of that thing way before prom."

I nodded so hard I accidentally conked my head on the pillar behind me. "I bet that's the plan! They're just being careful because they don't want to ruin the decorations."

I sighed happily. Except for the knot forming on the back of my head, I was feeling a million times better. I have a tendency to blow things way out of proportion sometimes, and this was obviously one of those times. Of course Sheriff Shifflett and Dr. Bruce weren't going to leave that thing up in the woods. Nobody would be that dumb. They were just working on a plan that they didn't want to share with a kid. I just needed to have a little faith.

The bell went off, so we got our stuff together and headed for biology. I have to admit, I was practically skipping down the hallway, that's how relieved I felt. It was like a huge load had been lifted off my back. I'd have to say something to Dr. Bruce later, just to let him know I was being 100 percent supportive.

But when I skipped into Dr. Bruce's class at the end of the hall, it was like a thousand-pound weight came crashing down onto my head. Dr. Bruce wasn't there. Bunny Smoody was.

She was standing at the front of the room practically twitching, she was so nervous, and her face was alternating between sweaty pink and throw-up white.

Ty and I stood wavering in the doorway, staring at her for what seemed like years before we staggered to our seats. I know we were rude, but we couldn't help it. It's not fun when your rationalizations get shredded by real life.

Bunny Smoody shot one last desperate glance at the door as the final bell rang. "What is it you kids are studying now? Something to do with nature?"

Nobody said a word. The corners of Bunny Smoody's mouth twitched like she was trying to smile. It wasn't working.

"Space, maybe? Is that it?"

You had to feel sorry for the woman. But I wasn't letting sentiment get in the way. I had to know. I stood up. "Where's Dr. Bruce?"

Bunny Smoody stared at me like my face had started melting into a puddle on the floor. Her lip even started quivering.

"Dr. Bruce? He—uh—"

"Was it that oboe convention?" Ty interrupted,

keeping his face completely straight. Honestly, to look at him, you'd think Dr. Bruce was the world's biggest oboe fan. "He was talking about it all last week."

Dr. Bruce had never mentioned an oboe in his life, but Bunny hopped on that like a puppy on a squeaky toy. "That's it! He is such a devotee of the oboe. That's where he is. The oboe convention."

Ty and I glanced at each other. We didn't need any more confirmation.

"Ms. Smoody," I said, heading for the door, "I'm sick. Can you walk me to the nurse?"

"Well . . ." Bunny Smoody hesitated. You could tell she was just itching to dash out the door, but subs aren't generally allowed to abandon their classes, even if they are married to the principal.

Ty raised his hand. "We were reading chapter twenty-seven, Ms. Smoody, if you want us to get started."

Bunny shot Ty another grateful look. Little did she know the book only went up to chapter twenty-three. Ty has no shame.

"Great. Do that, then. Read chapter twenty-seven, and I'll be right back."

I waited until Bunny Smoody had come out into the hallway and shut the door before I attacked.

"So what was left?" I asked, folding my arms. I wasn't wasting time with small talk. "Elbow? Big toe?"

Bunny's huge eyes brimmed with tears. "Two fingers," she whispered. "Just two fingers."

CHAPTER 10

HONESTLY, THERE ARE SOME THINGS YOU'RE JUST better off not knowing. I mean, a kid should not spend the afternoon trying to figure out which two fingers were left over when her science teacher got dissolved. It distracts you from your schoolwork, and I don't think it's good for your overall mental health.

I was a total wreck by the time I got home from school, and the worst part is, nobody even noticed. I dragged myself into the living room and flopped onto the squishy center of the couch, looking completely pathetic, and all

Mom did was ask me to move my feet so she could have more space to help with Tina's prom dress.

The house had been thrown into a minor frenzy earlier in the week when Señora Jenkins had suddenly announced that instead of the "Romance by the Lake" prom theme everybody had been planning on, the theme would now be "Spanish Showboat." Her rationale was that since her classes had been doing all the platform work, she should get to pick the theme. Principal Smoody was afraid that if he said no, she'd call a work stoppage. I saw that one coming a mile away, but apparently much of the school was stunned by the news.

Tina had promptly trashed her pink satiny prom dress, and she and Mom were in a frenzy trying to come up with a more Spanishy outfit.

I tucked my feet up underneath me so I wouldn't accidentally lose them in the prom frenzy and sighed heavily. A pair of big eyes blinked at me from under the bookshelf. I guess that whole "misery loves company" thing is true, because Mr. Boots crept out from his hiding place and huddled next to me on the couch. It was a bonding moment. He licked the seam of my blue jeans, and I brushed a clump of dust off the hem of his jaunty plaid skirt.

Mom came bustling back into the living room and scanned the room, looking for more stray feet, I'm guessing. "Are you going to be in here, Arlie? Because Tina's coming out in her dress."

I nodded. "I won't say anything." One wrong word about Tina's new dress could be disastrous. Someone could lose a head.

Mom smiled and patted me on the shoulder. "Good girl." She frowned at Mr. Boots and adjusted his little plaid cap, which had slipped over one eye. I swear, sometimes she's as bad as Tina.

Tina came clomping downstairs in her new outfit, and I have to say, it wasn't bad. She was wearing this bright red flamenco-ey number complete with black lace, ruffled hair clip, and little lace gloves. It gave her a kind of trashy señorita look, but on Tina, it worked.

She stomped into the middle of the room and looked

from me to Mom, daring us to say a word. Mr. Boots buried his face behind my feet. I didn't blame him.

"So?" Tina demanded. "What do you think?"

"It looks great," I said without thinking.

"Drop dead," Tina said, scowling.

"What?" I gasped. It was so unfair.

"Arlie, hush now. It looks precious!" Mom cooed. She couldn't have chosen a worse word. She seemed to realize that as soon as it left her mouth.

"Precious?" Tina looked vaguely disgusted, like she was about to rip the dress off and stomp it into the dust with her killing shoes.

"Mysterious. Sophisticated. Stylish. Marveloso," Mom said quickly. If she kept talking, she'd have to hit on the right adjective eventually.

One of those seemed to have done the job, because the wary look in Tina's eyes started to soften.

"Really?" she said, fanning out the skirt. "You think?"

Me and Mom both nodded like crazy. The prom was

only three days away. If Tina turned on this dress like she'd turned on the last one, Mom would have a nervous breakdown. At the rate I was going, though, she'd have to get in line.

Tina twirled a little and puffed up her sleeves. She looked happy enough that Mom attempted a risky maneuver. Us Jacobses are nothing if not daredevils. "Tina, honey?" she started. I held my breath. "Are those the shoes you're planning to wear?"

Tina looked down at her clumpy killing shoes. "Why? They go." Footwear has always been Tina's blind spot. It's her fashion Achilles heel.

Mom nodded so quickly she looked like one of those dashboard dogs driving over a gravel pit. "Of course, they're terrific. But I was just thinking . . . wait one second . . ."

Mom dashed into her bedroom. She came trotting back a couple of minutes later with a pair of black strappy high heels. "Try these!" she squealed. Mom was having way too much fun here.

"Are they yours?" Tina looked at the strappy shoes doubtfully.

"Never wore them. I can't think why I bought them," Mom said, tossing her head. Well, duh. Of course she bought them for Tina, and if Tina had half a brain she could've figured that out. Maybe the fact that Mom wears a size six and these were obviously a big honking, Tina-sized nine would've been a tip-off.

Tina rolled her eyes and kicked her clumpy shoes into the corner. She slipped on the strappy numbers, and I have to admit, it was like the shoes and the dress were fraternal twins separated at birth. Mom must have psychic fashion powers or something. Tina looked at the shoes with grudging admiration. It looked like we had an outfit.

That's when I decided to open my big fat mouth. I'm serious, I should move to one of those convents where they only let you talk once a day. Then maybe I'd do less damage.

"Are you going to be able to walk in those? It is at the lake, remember?"

Mom looked at me like I'd just shot out the windows and set the house on fire. "Oh, but . . . ," she chirped desperately.

"Yeah, it will be tough to walk in these," said Tina thoughtfully.

"Oh, but . . . ," Mom squeaked helplessly. I really felt bad, but there was nothing I could do. It was a little late to bite my tongue off.

"I mean, these heels are super spiky." Tina lifted one foot and inspected it carefully.

"Oh, but . . ." Looked like Mom's nervous break-down was moving up on the schedule.

"But who cares, right?" Tina said, her lips curling into an evil grin. "Trey will just have to drive me right up to the platform, won't he? Or carry me. How's that for an entrance?" Tina smirked happily. She was going for Prom Queen, and an entrance like that could only help her.

Mom practically sobbed with relief. "Perfect! It's all perfect."

She flopped down onto the couch next to Mr. Boots, making him bob up in the air like a Halloween apple. Tina stared at him in horror.

"Oh NO!" she shrieked. "Mr. Boots! What's he going to wear?"

Mr. Boots shrank back, turning almost as green as his little plaid outfit. Tina had been planning to use Mr. Boots as her prime accessory for the prom. She'd even gotten him a matching pink satin outfit with a big bow on the butt. He was supposed to look like a canine Marilyn Monroe.

"It's all RUINED!" Tina wailed.

Mom jumped up and patted Tina on the arm. "It's okay, honey. We'll get him a little mariachi outfit and he'll look terrific. You'll be the hit of the prom." Where she was going to find a dog-size mariachi outfit in three days was anybody's guess.

Tina sniffled and smiled at Mom. "Thanks, Mom. That'll be great." She really knows how to work it.

I didn't mention how pathetic it was that our dog was

going to the prom and I wasn't. Sure, I'm not really old enough, but heck, I'm older than Mr. Boots. It probably wouldn't have made any difference anyway.

"Now you go get changed, and we'll see what we can find for Mr. Boots, okay?" said Mom. Tina nodded and trotted upstairs in her new shoes.

Mom flopped back down on the couch. "Whoo! That was close, huh? But she's a darling, isn't she?"

I nodded and tried to smile, but my face felt frozen. I'd suddenly pictured Lake Heather swarming with kids. Sheriff Shifflett wouldn't be able to watch all of them.

I must've looked like death on a stick, because Mom finally noticed that something was up. She put her hand on my cheek. "What's wrong, Arlie? You and your little friend have a fight?"

I tested the waters. "I'm worried, Mom. There's something bad up at the lake."

Mom frowned, which was totally unlike her. She says facial movement causes wrinkles, which is why she generally tries to keep her face expression free at all times.

That's not to say she's successful, though. "Something bad? What do you mean?"

I took a deep breath and launched into it. "Something that killed Stacy Sizemore, Mom. She didn't fall into the quarry. A gummy thing got her. I heard Sheriff Shifflett talking about it. And it killed Howdy McDowell and Tammy Banks and Dr. Bruce, too. They can't have the prom there, not until it's gone. You've got to make them do something."

Mom stared at me for a second like her mental computer was running a little slow. "You heard Sheriff Shifflett talking? About something at the lake?"

"When I was at the dentist. And I've seen it. It's a monster. I know it's true."

Mom stared at me again, her perfect blank expression back on her face. Then she patted me on the leg and got up. "Well! I know somebody who's not watching any more scary movies. That imagination of yours is out of control."

"No, Mom—," I started, but she cut me off.

"Honey, all of us parents met with Sheriff Shifflett. He told us exactly what happened to the Sizemore girl. Now why would he lie to us, hmmm? Explain to me why." Mom folded her arms and stared at me like I was a pet mouse she'd caught munching the Cheez Whiz.

"I don't know why," I muttered.

"Exactly. And do you know why that is? Because he wouldn't." Mom crouched down and patted my knee again. "I know what happened with Stacy was scary. And I know you've imagined all sorts of horrible things. But you've got to realize, honey, it was an accident. Now are you sure this isn't about something else? Maybe you're just a little bit jealous about the prom? Do you think maybe a little part of you doesn't want Tina to go?"

Maybe a big part of me didn't want anybody to go. Not if they were going to turn up as leftovers the next morning. "I want her to go to the prom. Just not at the lake."

"Well, that's where it is. End of discussion." Mom looked up and smiled. Tina was standing at the foot of the stairs shooting death rays at the couch.

"Tina! All ready?" Mom patted her hair and trotted toward the bedroom. "Let me get my purse."

Tina waited until Mom had disappeared before storming up to the edge of the couch. I tried not to look at her. I didn't want my head to blow up.

"What, did you forget what I said?" Tina leaned over and hissed in my ear. Mr. Boots was pretending to be one of my feet, hoping Tina wouldn't notice I had an extra. "Don't you even think about ruining this prom for me, Arlie. Don't you *even*. I can manage things. There's nothing up there I can't handle. You didn't see anything, you got that?"

I didn't say anything, I just fiddled with Mr. Boots's hem. He growled at me for blowing his cover.

"You got that?" Tina demanded again.

"Got it," I muttered.

"You better," Tina hissed, straightening up and pretending to look at a magazine just as Mom came back out with her purse.

"Bye, Arlie, we'll be back soon," Mom called in to

me. Tina was still wearing the strappy shoes, and Mom smiled at them happily. "Now, Tina, you be sure Trey drives you up to the platform, because you're right, those heels will sink right into the dirt."

"I will," said Tina, smiling again. Abusing Trey always brightened her day.

I gave a halfhearted wave as they drove away, but Mom's last words echoed in my ears. Suddenly all I could see was an image of Stacy Sizemore, hot pink heels sunk deep in the ground as a slimy gummy tentacle slithered toward her. You didn't have to be stupid or slow. You just had to be stuck. And in three days, almost every girl in school would be up there, perfumed to the gills, with heels sinking deep into the mud.

CHAPTER 11

"LUNCH MEAT," TY SAID FOR ABOUT THE MIL-
lionth time that morning. Ever since I'd told
him my theory about the high heels, it was
what he'd been labeling every girl who walked
by. It was starting to get on my nerves, to tell
the truth. Even though I pretty much agreed
with him. Any girl who went to that prom had
about a fifty-fifty chance of ending up as table
scraps.

"Lunch meat," said Ty, nodding to Donna
Cavillari as she walked by. Donna shot him a
nasty look and whispered something to Marty

Bollinger. This situation was not doing wonders for our social lives. Nobody was going to want to hang around with the crazy "lunch meat" twins.

"Shut up, Ty. It's not helping," I finally said, trying to ignore the warning bell that was blasting away.

"So what. Nothing does," he grumbled. Ty had tried telling his parents about the thing at the lake last night too, with even worse results. His parents had laughed their butts off at first, and then, when they realized he wasn't kidding, they'd gotten super concerned. He has an appointment with a therapist next week.

I picked myself up and trudged off toward Spanish class. Me and Ty were just going to have to face it: Our lives had turned into huge piles of reeking garbage. I tried to buck myself up as I walked. It couldn't get any worse, right?

I was actually starting to believe that until I turned the corner and saw Señora Jenkins waiting for me. I wasn't just being paranoid, either. She was focused on me like her eyes were set on tractor beam. I didn't know what her problem was, because I wasn't even late or any-thing.

I hesitated outside of the classroom, Señora Jenkins glaring at me from the middle of the doorway. I'm not sure what she expected me to do. Unless I wanted to scoot my books between her legs and crawl around her feet, there was no way I was getting into that classroom. I'm not made of Silly Putty, you know.

"I'm not late yet," I said. It's okay for teachers to bust you when you get to class late—I expect that. But it's no fair for them to make you late on purpose just to ream you out.

Señora Jenkins didn't seem to care about such minor technicalities. She jerked her head in the direction of the main hallway. "Arlene. Office. Now," she barked.

I learned a long time ago that arguing with Señora Jenkins is pretty pointless, but I wasn't about to give up so easily. It would stink if the one thing I ended up get-ting detention for was the one thing I hadn't even done. I rolled my eyes and oozed attitude.

"But—," I started.

"Now!" Señora Jenkins totally ignored me. She just folded her arms and waited. Carla Tate and Mitzi Chang were at their desks, craning their necks to catch all the action. At least my horrible life had some entertainment value.

"Okay, but—," I tried again. I didn't even try the attitude this time. Attitude only works when the person you're talking to is actually listening.

Señora Jenkins didn't even answer me. She just gave me a shove in the direction of the office.

"Fine." So I was depriving my classmates of the most excitement to hit Spanish class all week. I didn't care anymore. I didn't even have the strength to argue. The late bell blasted overhead as I headed toward the office. I had had it with this lousy school.

The pinch-faced office lady whose name I can never remember pursed her mouth at me like I was some hardened criminal and immediately scurried away into the dark reaches of the school office. Most of the time when you get sent down there, they leave you waiting in the glass-enclosed outer office for hours, to humiliate you as much as possible, I guess. I was just settling down for a couple of uninterrupted hours of alone time when she hurried back in and hustled me into Principal Smoody's private office. Through his private door.

Nobody goes in through the private door.

Principal Smoody was sitting behind his desk, wringing his meaty hands. He grimaced when I came in, like the sight of me made him feel woozy.

"Close the door, please, Ms. Skinner," Principal Smoody said. Ms. Skinner. I'd have to remember that. But as the door closed behind me, I realized I had bigger problems than just a bad memory or chronic lateness. I was trapped in my worst school-scented nightmare.

Principal Smoody stared at me for a moment, his eyes half-closed. He didn't even offer me a chair or anything. It looked like he'd gone into a trance. I didn't say anything to interrupt him. A trance would be fine by me. I slid my books to the floor by the door and tried to act casual.

"You spoke to my wife yesterday, did you not?" Principal Smoody finally said. His voice sounded flat and calm, like he was working really hard to control it.

I shrugged. "She subbed for my class."

"My wife has been under a lot of pressure lately, Arlene. Does that mean anything to you?" Principal Smoody opened his eyes wide and glared at me.

"That's too bad," I said slowly. I was beginning to see what this was all about. That Bunny was such a snitch. It wasn't my fault she'd spilled the beans about Dr. Bruce.

Principal Smoody made a weird rumbling noise for a couple of minutes before exploding. "For God's sake, Arlene! Didn't you learn anything from Sheriff Shifflett's speech the other day? Didn't you?" Little beads of sweat popped up on his forehead.

Trust me to be the wise guy. "Yeah, it was great. But we learned how to cross the street in elementary school, Principal Smoody."

Principal Smoody looked like he was about to lunge over the edge of the desk and beat me to death with his day planner. "Gossip, young lady! Taking advantage of your substitute like that, pumping her for information, spreading filthy rumors. It's unconscionable."

Something inside me snapped. I'd had it up to here with the lectures. Chances were, I already had detention for the next twenty years just for making Bunny cry, so what difference would another ten years make? I laid it on the line.

"No, what's unconscionable is that there's a huge monster at the lake eating your students and you won't do anything about it." I leaned against the wall and let Principal Smoody chew on that one for a couple of minutes.

Principal Smoody sat back in his chair and tried to regain his sleepy superior pose, but he couldn't quite do it. His ears went bright pink and his nostrils twitched. "I have no knowledge of any such monster."

Oh, please. I rolled my eyes. "You don't? It's the one

that ate Dr. Bruce. That's what freaked Bunny out, not me. I just happened to ask about it."

Principal Smoody looked at his day planner carefully, like he might have a surprise appointment with the Publishers Clearing House prize patrol any minute.

"Dr. Bruce's absence has nothing to do with any creature," he said carefully. "The only reason Bunny jumped to that conclusion was because of your malicious gossip." He closed the planner and sat back in his chair. "It is my understanding that the creature is nothing more than an oversize carp."

"A carp." I still don't know if Principal Smoody actually believed Shifflett's carp story, but I wasn't about to let him off that easy.

"Great. It's a carp, then," I agreed. "Let's just say it's a great big honking carp." I tried to control my voice and sound calm. Principal Smoody was too stupid to live. I hoped he was planning to chaperone the prom. "Well, I saw your carp dissolve a frog with its tentacle. Got any problems with that?"

Principal Smoody's left cheek twitched for a second. "Students will not be swimming during the prom," he finally said.

"This carp hangs out on land."

Principal Smoody stared at me for a long minute and then lunged toward the intercom on his desk. "Students, this is Principal Smoody speaking." He cleared his throat and nodded at me. "I would like to make an announcement regarding the prom this weekend. Fishermen have spotted an unusually large carp in the lake, but we have been assured it is completely harmless. If you don't bother it, it won't bother you. Please respect nature and the environment during the festivities this weekend. Thank you."

Principal Smoody clicked off the intercom and smiled at me. "There, that takes care of that. I'm not going to suspend you now, Arlene. But if you insist on perpetuating these unfortunate rumors about Dr. Bruce, I will be forced to take action. Do you understand?"

"High heels stick in the mud, Principal Smoody.

Somebody will get trapped. Somebody will get dissolved."

Principal Smoody's face turned bright red as he jabbed his finger onto the intercom button again. "This is Principal Smoody. If you do *not* respect nature this weekend, the prom will be canceled. Thank you."

He folded his arms and smiled smugly at me. "And that, Arlene, is the best I can do."

It was then that Principal Smoody remembered to click off the intercom.

It was like all my insides had suddenly rushed down into the soles of my feet. It didn't matter what happened at the prom now. Thanks to Principal Smoody and that lousy intercom, I wasn't going to live to see it. Not now that the whole school knew I was responsible.

"Now I expect you to do the best you can do," Principal Smoody continued, like he hadn't just totally destroyed my life. "Understood?"

I just stared at him. Like there was anything to say.

Apparently I must've had some kind of surly look on

my face, because the principal suddenly lurched forward over the desk, his face bright red. Seriously, I was thinking heart attack.

"Think of my position here, Arlene," Smoody hissed at me, his eyes bulging. "Sheriff Shifflett has personally assured me that everything is fine. So I have to assume that everything really is fine." Little flecks of spit were collecting in the corners of his mouth. "He's on the school board, Arlie. . . ."

He stared at me with a pleading look in his eyes, reminding me in a weird way of Mr. Boots. Thinking about it, it had been a pretty rough year for Principal Smoody, what with the Mayonnaise Festival fiasco and that incident where the work crews digging up the school time capsule accidentally ruptured the school septic tank. I decided to cut the guy a break. What difference did it make, anyway? He wasn't going to budge. Detention wouldn't even be worth the trouble.

I nodded. "Understood."

Principal Smoody nodded back and waved me toward

the door. I scooped up my books and scurried out of his private door into the hallway. I looked around nervously. If I ran, maybe I could make it to the bikes before the bell rang.

That bell hates me, I swear. Because as soon as I thought that, the warning bell jangled overhead and tons of students poured into the hallway.

And leading the pack was none other than Tina. Sometimes I think I was implanted with a homing device at birth, because Tina never has any trouble finding me when she's pissed. And boy, was she pissed now. Steam was practically coming out of her ears. She made a beeline for me, slamming into kids left and right as she stormed down the hall.

I turned and escaped around the corner into the main hallway. I'd have to think of an excuse later. Right now, all that mattered was survival.

The main hallway was the worst choice I could've made, though. There, in the entryway, was Sheriff Shifflett. He was holding a bunch of RE-ELECT SHERIFF

SHIFFLETT posters, and it was obvious from the look on his face that he'd heard the announcement too. Steam wasn't just coming out of his ears. It was coming out of every opening imaginable. I had one thought—escape. I would've gotten away no problem, I'm convinced, but I turned so fast that I slipped on some kid's lost home-work. When I looked up, Sheriff Shifflett was standing over me.

"Office. NOW," he barked, scowling at me.

I got up and headed back into the office, the sheriff right behind me.

"Out, Smoody," he bellowed when we got through the door, and he pushed me into Principal Smoody's pri-vate office. Principal Smoody hopped to his feet, nod-ding and yessing like a bobblehead as he gathered his papers and scurried out. Sheriff Shifflett sat behind the desk and stared at me for what had to be the longest minute of my life.

"You think I'm a fool, girl? Is that what you think?"

Honestly, I don't know why people ask questions like that. I mean, come on, what do they expect you to say? Yes?

"No."

"Then you need to stop poking your nose in where it don't belong. I'm the sheriff. I know about the situation at the lake. I've been keeping things quiet, that's true, but I've got the situation in hand."

"But the monster——," I started, but Sheriff Shifflett cut me off.

"I know what Bruce was saying," Shifflett snorted, "all up in arms over a few mutations or whatnot. Mutant fish, frogs with five legs, that sort of thing. That's not what we're talking here."

I nodded, feeling relieved. Sheriff Shifflett knew about the creature. "Then you know? It got Howdy and Tammy and the rest."

Sheriff Shifflett smoothed his hair back. "Now whoa there, girl. We don't have a monster at the lake eating kids, that's just the gossip. When you get older, you learn to separate the facts from the fairy tales. No, what we have here is a bona fide killer, and you'll be glad to know, I arrested him this morning."

I could only gape at him. "But I saw—"

"I've been up there every day, gathering evidence, watching over you kids. And maybe I should've said straight out what we were dealing with, but the last thing this town needs is a huge panic. So I watched and waited and this morning I arrested Jeremiah Jones."

I just stared at him. Jeremiah Jones? Who the heck was that? "You arrested this Jones guy for murder?"

Sheriff Shifflett nodded. "Right now, I got him on creating a public disturbance, harassment, and public nudity, but he's the culprit, no doubt, and I'll be charging him with the murders soon. When my case is rock solid." He chuckled. "At a more, let's say, politically advantageous time."

It was the public nudity that tipped me off. I gasped. "The Walker? You arrested him? But he was trying to warn us."

175

"Jeremiah Jones, aka the Walker, that's him. Real clever the way he fixed it to make things seem all mysterious. Almost had me going for a minute there. But we got him cold. He was in the area, harassing those kids, he has a history of mental imbalance—heck, I even caught him with the gold belt that one of those little missies was wearing. Now I'm only telling you this because you seem to think you're some kind of little detective. Well, you're done, mystery solved."

Sheriff Shifflett got up and smoothed back his hair again. He looked pretty satisfied with himself. "This is our secret, you hear? Just know, there's nothing up there that'll hurt a hair on those kids at the prom."

I tried to swallow, but my throat wasn't cooperating.

"So we all done here? We've got an understanding?"

I nodded again and headed for the door. As soon as my feet hit the hallway, I took off running.

"Hey, Arlie, respect the fish! Or you'll get a cold, slimy fin smack on the kisser!" Marty Bollinger laughed as I skittered by.

Sheriff Shifflett was right—gossip was a horrible thing. And if I hadn't seen it with my own eyes, I might even think his theory was true. But this time the horrible thing was that the gossip was right.

CHAPTER 12

YOU CAN PRETTY MUCH GUESS WHAT THE REST
of my week was like. I've never heard so many
carp jokes in my life. If I didn't think half of the
comedians ribbing me would be hors d'oeuvres
by Sunday morning, it would've been unbear-
able.

"Better make sure Tina wears sensible
shoes," Ty said gloomily as he packed up his
books Friday afternoon. I nodded. Not that it
would be easy. Ever since she'd gotten those
strappy numbers, Tina had practically been
living in them. It would take a crowbar to get

them off her feet, but it was worth a try. I think Dad had one in the trunk.

The prom was the next day, and things couldn't be bleaker. Ever since the intercom fiasco, it had been close to impossible for me to go scope out the scene at the lake. Even if Tina and Sheriff Shifflett hadn't been keeping tabs on my every move, the "fish girl" couldn't set foot near Lake Heather without being subjected to an embarrassing comedy routine. I could take the heat, but it made any secret operations pretty much impossible. And it's tough to exterminate a slimy gummy monster long distance.

Ty gave me a halfhearted wave and took off on his bike. I'd never felt more helpless in my life. My big plan for the rest of the weekend was to go home and forget about the prom, but Mr. Boots wasn't making it easy for me. I had just settled in for a fun afternoon of holding back tears when he came skittering in wearing a huge mariachi hat and bolero jacket with his little plaid skirt. He was also wearing a horrified expression on his face. I'm guessing he'd just seen himself in the mirror.

"Arlie, is that you?" Mom trotted out holding a pair of little doggie-size pants with intricate embroidery up the legs and around the tail hole. Mr. Boots immediately took cover under the coffee table. "I've got to go to the store for more embroidery thread. You'll watch Mr. Boots while I'm gone, won't you?"

I shrugged and heaved myself up from the couch. I didn't want to deal with either of them. "Sure, whatever," I called back over my shoulder. It wasn't like I had anything better to do. Besides, how hard is it to keep an eye on a dog weighed down under a huge hat? He'd be too embarrassed to go anywhere, and even if he tried, he wouldn't be able to move very fast.

I opened the front door to go mope on the stoop for a while, and immediately reeled back in shock. There, on the steps, was an alien.

Okay, on second glance it wasn't exactly an alien. It was Ty in his old yellow snowsuit with gardening gloves and huge ski goggles on. But hey, anybody can make a mistake, right?

Ty took off the goggles and grinned at me. "Get your snowsuit. I've got a plan."

I hesitated for a second. Not that the idea of getting all decked out in my ancient snowsuit wasn't appealing, but a tiny little part of me wanted to know why the heck we were doing it.

Ty rolled his eyes and snapped his goggles back in place. "Just trust me, okay?" He sighed.

It was like I was suddenly filled with helium. We were going to do something. It didn't matter that the use of snowsuits in May suggested that Ty's plan was going to be incredibly lame. I was all for it, even if it meant wearing flippers on my head and marshmallows in my ears. It was definitely better than sitting around embroidering pants for a dog.

I rooted around in the hall closet for a couple of minutes and managed to unearth my old red snowsuit, a snorkeling mask complete with snorkel, and some metallic-looking reflective gloves.

Ty detached the snorkel and handed the mask back

to me. "This is great!" he enthused while I climbed into the snowsuit. The theory was that if we wore the snow-suits and gear while we implemented Ty's master plan, it would protect us from any accidental contact with an unfriendly tentacle. I just hoped the actual plan would be better than the outfits. Snowsuits in May are only fun for a couple of minutes, tops.

Ty filled me in on his plan while I adjusted the mask and gloves. I have to admit, it was a terrific idea. I just hoped we could pull it off.

Mr. Boots was watching us from his hiding place under the coffee table, and I'm serious, he was shaking so hard I thought he was going to make himself sick. I think he was trying not to laugh. I glared at him from behind my snorkel mask. Dogs in mariachi outfits have no right to laugh at people in snowsuits and swim gear.

We had just gotten ourselves all fixed up when Mom came hurrying in with her purse. She didn't even blink when she saw us. It made me wonder how weird Mom thinks I really am.

"Are you planning on going out, hon?" she said, adjusting her earrings.

"Yeah." I pulled the mask up so I could see her better. My breath was fogging it up pretty badly. Either that, or it was the steam seeping out of my collar. I was already starting to feel sweaty and gross.

"Well, remember to take Mr. Boots with you. I want you to keep an eye on him." Mom patted me on the back and adjusted the collar of my snowsuit.

"But Mom . . . ," I whined. Mr. Boots would totally mess up the plan.

"Just snap on his Flexi leash," Mom said, trotting out the door. "You won't even notice he's there."

Ty groaned as she shut the door. "Do we have to?"

Mr. Boots had stopped shaking and was staring at us with a stricken expression. Ty stared down at him doubtfully. Mr. Boots blinked, making the little tassels on his hat shake. The full mariachi effect was pretty staggering.

"Is that what he's going to wear? I mean, he looks

kind of funny," Ty said. I didn't point out that Ty wouldn't exactly blend in with the crowd himself.

"I think she forgot he was still dressed up," I said, inspecting Mr. Boots's embroidered sleeve. He'd probably get all messed up at the lake, but I didn't feel like finding him a new top to put on. "Come on, Mr. Boots," I said, dragging him out from under the table by his armpits. "Just hang back and try to stay out of the mud. Everything should be okay."

I hadn't really realized how weird we all looked until we headed out and climbed on our bikes. Ty was balancing a huge plastic sack on his knees while he rode, and I had Mr. Boots squealing in my basket.

I pushed my mask farther up on my forehead so I could see, but it didn't make me look any more normal. We didn't look like aliens anymore. We looked like two nuclear power plant workers kidnapping a hysterical mariachi dog from the rest of his band. I just hoped we wouldn't attract too much attention.

Amazingly, nobody really seemed to notice us much.

Well, okay, they totally noticed us, but nobody said anything or even seemed to care. Maybe we looked more official than I thought.

We ditched our bikes at the foot of the path at the lake, and attempted to amble nonchalantly past the frenzied last-minute prom work. I don't know why we bothered, though. I swear, the gummy monster could've strolled up and asked for a glass of lemonade and somebody would've just handed him a hammer. Amber Vanderklander was almost in tears trying to loop white Christmas lights around the railing of the platform. I sighed in relief. No carp jokes this time. We had work to do.

Once we'd ducked behind the trees, Ty started unloading his plastic bag. Inside, he had two of the biggest Super Soakers I'd ever seen. They were also two of the leakiest I'd ever seen. They were filled to the brim with some dangerous-looking greenish liquid. Ty handed me the barfy hot pink one, and kept the cool lime green one for himself. I bit my tongue and didn't say anything. If he wanted to be selfish at a time like this, fine.

"So what's in here, anyway?" I asked, trying to avoid touching whatever was dripping out of the nozzle of my Super Soaker.

"Mine's filled with undiluted weed killer, the heavy-duty stuff," Ty said, his eyes gleaming behind his goggles. "My dad had a lot left over from his dandelion war last summer. You're supposed to mix it with water, but I figure it's stronger this way."

"I don't think the thing's a plant, Ty," I said. Not to burst his bubble.

"That's why yours is filled with bug spray." Ty grinned. He really had thought of everything.

I nodded and shoved my mask down over my face. I felt a giddy rush of power. We were actually doing it. So what if nobody cared or believed us? We could do it ourselves. That gummy thing was history. Nothing could withstand a double dose of poison.

We crept closer to the edge of the water, Super Soakers up and ready, dragging Mr. Boots along behind us. The hem of his little plaid skirt was getting covered with mud, but except for a couple of stray flecks of ooze, his bolero jacket and hat were still clean. Too late to worry about it now, I figured—I'd just have to hope nobody noticed the skirt. I gave the Flexi leash another tug and headed deeper into the woods.

When we were a couple of feet from the water, we stopped and looked around. The place seemed deserted. I scanned the ground for any unusually heavy patches of slime, but the only sign of the monster was that frog's leftover flipper. I shuddered and scanned the trees, like I expected the monster to be hovering overhead or building a nest. It was pointless, I know. But the last thing I wanted to do was accidentally spot Dr. Bruce's finger.

Ty pulled his goggles off and looked around. Sweat was streaming down his face, and he had big indent marks where the goggles had been. "I don't see it."

I shook my head. I didn't see anything either. "Maybe it only comes out at night? Too many people around? Too much noise or something? I don't know."

Ty shrugged and wandered around like a kid lost at

the mall. "What if we can't find it?" he whined.

I started to get cranky. Apparently, part of Ty's master plan was for the monster to jump out with a big bull's-eye on its chest shouting, "Shoot me! Shoot me!" or something.

"We've got to find it," I said. "We'll just wait here till we do." We had twenty-four hours until the prom, and I was willing to sit there all night if I had to. The only one who'd really be missed was Mr. Boots, and I doubted he'd mind missing out on his last fitting session.

Mr. Boots must've suddenly smelled something really interesting, because he stuck his head right into a scrubby bush nearby. He got so involved with whatever it was that he caught his little hat string on a branch in there and couldn't get out. The only reason I even noticed was because of the loud choking noises coming from behind me.

I put down my Super Soaker and dragged Mr. Boots out by the butt. His little face had gone purple, and the string to his hat was all tangled up. I freed his hat from the recesses of the bush and plopped it back on his head, loosely looping the neck string over the brim. Mr. Boots gagged again thankfully and tottered sideways over toward Ty.

"Arlie . . . ," Ty gasped, stepping backward and almost creaming Mr. Boots. There, by the lake, was the monster.

I'd been looking there just a couple of minutes before, and I swear it hadn't been there. But it must've been, right? How could I miss a huge, slimy blob?

I scrambled for my Super Soaker, and me and Ty both took aim. But before either of us could even pull the trigger, it happened. That tentacle, that slow-moving slimy wormy thing, whipped out with lightning speed. Ty and I reeled back as the tentacle whipped between us and snatched the huge mariachi hat right off Mr. Boots's head.

I didn't think that dog's eyes could bulge out any farther, but apparently I was wrong. Mr. Boots sucked in his breath so hard that he literally sucked a leaf right off the ground and into his mouth.

We were way out of our league here. We'd completely underestimated this thing. It was no slow-moving piece of solidified slime. It was a speedy and hungry killer. And it hadn't eaten in days.

I scooped Mr. Boots up so fast that I didn't quite grab him right. He was dangling by his front legs as I tucked him under my arm and took aim again. We couldn't afford to miss. We had to kill this thing.

Almost at the same time, me and Ty pulled on the triggers of our Super Soakers. Two fast, heavy blasts of liquid went streaming toward the gummy monster, hitting it right in the middle section and on the tentacle. The monster reeled back, quivering under the force of the poison. It jiggled just like a Jell-O mold, but I forced the image out of my mind. Jell-O's a personal favorite of mine, and an association like that is one thing I don't need.

We kept pumping the poison out for almost a full minute, until our Super Soakers were completely empty. Then we stepped back to see what would happen.

The monster was glistening with liquid, and it continued to shake even after we'd stopped shooting. I let out a long, jagged sigh. Nothing could withstand that. The leaves around the thing were already looking severely unhappy.

Then suddenly I heard it—a low, rumbling, sucking sound. As we watched, the monster sucked up every drop of the liquid until it was dry as a bone. And the worst part was, it looked like it was getting bigger.

"Ty . . . ," I tried to say, but my throat wouldn't let me. It didn't feel like talking. It felt like screaming.

We dropped our Super Soakers and scrambled back through the trees. We didn't even stop running when we got to our bikes—we just scooped them up and ran with them until we could hop on and ride away.

It wasn't until we'd made it to the gas station just outside town that we finally stopped.

"We are so screwed," Ty gasped, leaning on his handlebars.

Mr. Boots was still dangling from under my arm, and

I dropped him onto the pavement, where he collapsed in a shivering heap. His huge tasseled hat was gone, and little spots of weed killer were bleaching out his black bolero jacket.

I unzipped my snowsuit and flopped down next to him on the pavement. I was soaking wet with sweat, but my teeth were practically chattering, I felt so cold.

"Nobody can stop that thing," I said, shaking my head. I couldn't believe we'd been so wrong about the gummy monster. There weren't going to be one or two missing kids after the prom was over. After what I'd just seen, I wasn't sure there were going to be any kids left at all.

CHAPTER 13

THE FIRST THING I DID WHEN I GOT HOME WAS turn on Mr. Boots. Personally, I blame Mom for making it so easy.

"Mr. Boots!" Mom shrieked as we walked through the door. "What have you done to your outfit?"

I unclipped the Flexi leash, and Mr. Boots went streaking through the living room and down into the basement. I felt bad sacrificing the little guy, sure, but I was in no mood to explain how he'd gotten so messed up. I didn't want to end up in the cell next to Ty's at the loony bin.

"He got loose when we were out. He ate the little hat and was starting on the jacket when we caught up to him. I couldn't stop him. He was out of control." I could hear Mr. Boots cussing me out from the basement. I tried to ignore him.

Mom and Tina both gasped in horror. Mr. Boots was lucky he'd already made his escape. I don't know what they would have done if they'd caught him right then. Bad things happen to dogs who eat their clothes. Mr. Boots must've sensed this, because he wasn't taking any chances. We didn't see him again until early Saturday afternoon.

Mom looked mournfully at the little embroidered pants in her hands. "I don't know if I can make another hat and jacket in time, Tina," she said, her lips quivering.

Tina snatched the little pants away and flung them onto the floor. "That little rat doesn't deserve to go to the prom. He can just suck it up and stay home," she spat in disgust.

Mom blinked back tears. "Are you sure, honey? Because if I worked all night . . ."

"Forget it, Mom. He'd just be a third wheel anyway." Tina polished a spot on her strappy shoes and tripped off to her room to look at her dress again. I tripped off to my room to be sick.

Tomorrow was going to be a nightmare, and there was nothing I could do. Me and Ty had given it our best shot, and we'd totally failed. I didn't even want to think about what was going to happen at the lake tomorrow with all those unsuspecting kids parading around like corn dogs at a ballgame.

At least Tina wouldn't be one of them, not if I could help it, anyway. Since I couldn't keep her home, I figured the key to saving her would be to keep her mobile, meaning those strappy heels had to go. After everybody had gone to sleep, I snuck into Tina's bathroom, hid her perfume, and went to work scraping away at one of the heels with the little emery board I found in her drawer. It didn't achieve the totally lopsided effect I was going for, but they were definitely uneven. There was no way she could wear them now without lurching around like a drunken sailor. And somehow, I don't think that's the look she was going for.

The next day was pretty much a horrible blur. The high point for me came when I first woke up and found out Mr. Boots had some backbone after all. At some point during the night, he had attacked the mariachi pants and strung the remains through the living room and dining room and into the bathroom, where I think he attempted to flush them. It went perfectly with the story I'd cooked up for Mom, so I didn't mind in the least. Having used up the last of his backbone, Mr. Boots spent the rest of the morning wisely hiding under the bookshelf.

The rest of the day was a total Tina-fest, complete with every prom-related crisis imaginable. Mr. Boots and his ruined mariachi suit couldn't even compare with one o'clock's terrible black vs. nude hose battle (nude was declared victorious) or four o'clock's clumpy nail polish tragedy. I tried to follow Mr. Boots's example and stay out of the way. I didn't want to be in the line of fire when Tina noticed what had happened to her shoes.

But, weirdly enough, the explosion never happened. Every time I heard Tina screaming, I would guiltily prick up my ears, but some other accessory was always the culprit. Finally I got so sick of waiting for it that I threw myself on the bomb.

"So how're the shoes?" I asked as Tina curled her bangs.

"Get out," Tina barked at me, trying to make a little piece of hair curl on her cheek. Trey had been downstairs waiting for Tina for the past ten minutes, so it was pretty discouraging to see the strappy shoes already firmly on her feet.

"Working for you, then?" I persisted.

"GET OUT!" Tina screamed at the top of her lungs. "MOM!"

I didn't wait for Mom. I ran downstairs so fast I almost slid into the living room on the area rug. "She's almost ready," I said, flopping into a chair. I don't know what I was so nervous about. She wouldn't be able to take two steps in those shoes.

But when Tina came down, I almost swallowed my gum. Except for a couple of bobbles on the stairs, she was trotting around like her legs had been uneven all her life. She was even managing to balance Mr. Boots on her shoulder, which was a trick in itself. Tina had been so pleased with the resolution of the five o'clock mousse fiasco that she'd given him a doggie spa treatment and gotten him all decked out in last year's gold lamé Oscar outfit. He still wasn't getting to go to the prom, though. Not that I heard Mr. Boots complaining.

Tina and Trey posed for pictures with Mr. Boots and Tootie, who was sporting a snazzy lace bow for the occasion. My stomach churned as Mom snapped pictures and Dad tried not to burst a blood vessel. I didn't know where I'd gone wrong. I was so sure the heels were uneven.

I don't think it really hit me until I'd watched them drive away. Tina was even more of a sitting duck than

Tootie was. Escaping in the strappy shoes would've been difficult before. Now, thanks to me, it would be downright impossible.

"I've just killed my sister," I said when Ty called a couple of minutes later. I took the phone into the other room first, though. Mom and Dad didn't need to hear something like that.

"Seriously?" said Ty.

"Might as well have." I told him about the shoes.

"Man, that stinks," Ty said, whistling softly. "She's toast. Well, look on the bright side. She'll have company. How many do you think it'll get, thirty, forty percent of the class? For munchies, I mean."

"Shut up, Ty." It wasn't funny.

"Because it's going to do some serious damage up there, Arlie."

"I know that, okay? But what are we supposed to do?" I was getting so sick of going over this. We'd lost. We just needed to face it and hope we still had some classmates left on Monday.

"I just think we should be there, that's all."

I rolled my eyes. You can only go to the prom if you're a junior or senior or dating a junior or senior. Neither one of us qualified. "We can't, remember? And it's a little late, even if we could."

"I don't mean officially."

I was starting to catch on. "You think we should just go up there? Why, so we can watch? You're sick, you know that?"

"Not to watch, to keep watch. Make sure it stays on the right side of the lake. You know, to warn them, go for help, that kind of thing."

"Oh." It did make a certain kind of sense. It couldn't hurt. And after the way I'd just sabotaged Tina, it might be worth a shot. "Okay. Meet me in ten minutes."

Mom and Dad were hanging out in the living room, smiling at me expectantly as I came downstairs. It gave me a funny feeling. I smiled back and hurried toward the door, trying to make it out without further eye contact. It didn't work.

"Arlie, wait," Mom said, standing up. "Are you going out somewhere?"

I should've known I'd be busted. I nodded and shrugged casually. "Just hanging out with Ty."

Mom smiled her most maternal and guilt-inducing smile. "Mr. Boots looks so beautiful. You wouldn't mind . . ." She blinked her eyes at me pleadingly. Mr. Boots eyed the basement door. It was shut. We were both trapped.

"Mom, no. He looks great, but it really isn't—"

"It would mean so much to him. He's so disappointed about missing the prom. He needs a night out." Mom beamed and hooked Mr. Boots up to the Flexi leash. "Just don't let him ruin the outfit."

I groaned. This could not be happening again. But apparently it was, because the next thing I knew, I had an armful of squirmy gold lamé Chihuahua. Ty was not going to be pleased.

He wasn't. He took one look at us waiting out front and shook his head. "You know, lamé without the accent mark is just lame," he said. Ty can be so darn cool some-times. It's enough to make you puke.

Mr. Boots glared at Ty and shook his head, making a little puff of rose-scented doggie powder float into the air. I groaned. My perfume theory had better be wrong, or we were in deep trouble.

By the time Ty finished grousing about Mr. Boots and Mr. Boots finished whining about the bike ride, I was just about ready to chuck them both to the gummy monster and write the whole night off as a loss. But what we saw up at the lake snapped us all out of our foul moods.

I'm serious, one look at that platform was enough to make you bust out laughing. Not to be mean or anything. For a creaky wooden platform on a putrid, stinky lake, it looked amazingly good. You couldn't even tell that it was leaning to one side that much. We had a pretty clear view from our hiding place on the path, too. Amber had managed to get all the sparkly Christmas lights draped around the railings just right, and there were all kinds of piñatas and colorful hangings draped on posts. It looked festive, even. It wasn't the platform that really cracked us up, though—it was the people.

Principal Smoody, for one. He was dancing. Not just regular dancing either, but dancing by himself with his eyes shut tight, one hand on his stomach and one hand waving in the air. Tina was standing right next to him, and I don't know how she managed to keep it together. She sucked down one of those nonalcoholic margaritas at lightning speed and then wobbled over and sucked down the one Trey was holding. I think it was the only way she could keep from laughing.

Bunny Smoody was hovering in the corner of the platform with the enormous margarita machine. She was cranking them out like crazy, dipping the glasses in salt and decorating them with all kinds of huge umbrellas and plastic frogs. Tina had been raving about how great the fake margaritas were going to be all week long, but I think the real reason they were such a big hit was because the music was so lame. I mean, let's face it, it was a tape player. The one from Señora Jenkins's classroom.

Señora Jenkins was guarding it like a disco-loving junkyard dog, swaying and snapping her fingers as she alternated among Spanish folk music, obscure disco hits, and Lionel Richie, sometimes alone, sometimes with the Commodores. Kids were lurching around on the uneven platform, attempting to dance, I guess, but nobody seemed overly thrilled by the selection. I sensed a coup in the making.

After a couple of minutes of unrestrained floor rolling and knee slapping, me and Ty pulled ourselves together and remembered what we were there for. I wiped my eyes and scanned the slimy side of the lake. It was totally still.

"See anything?" Ty asked, peering around the dark path.

"Nope," I said. Maybe Lionel Richie had driven the gummy thing away. I squinted across the lake at the trees. I couldn't even see any slime. Not that I was disappointed, but spending the night just watching somebody else's prom wasn't really my idea of a good time. I reminded myself of the alternative and tried to get into the music.

At least Mr. Boots seemed to be enjoying himself. He was doing a thorough inspection of every inch of the path, rock by rock. He even tasted a couple. I let out the Flexi leash a little bit and let him go to it. He doesn't get out much.

I hugged my knees and glanced back at the platform just in time to see Principal Smoody confiscate Tina's fake margarita and sniff it. I stifled a giggle. The drunken sailor effect was working wonderfully, but I don't think I could take all the credit. That platform was making everybody stagger around like they'd just taken their Rollerblades off.

Principal Smoody realized his mistake too late to escape Tina's wrath. Her face went red with righteous indignation, and whipping the strappy shoes off her feet, she stormed over to the edge of the platform, stalked out into the grass, and took careful aim at something. I peered over to see what she was aiming at. It was Trey's convertible. Trey hadn't been able to drive right up to the platform, apparently—he'd had to park about half-way between the platform and our hiding place. Ten bucks says she made him carry her, though.

Shooting daggers at Principal Smoody, Tina chucked the shoes into the backseat with a clang. You'd think Trey would've cleaned out some of the junk in his car for the prom, but from the sound of that clang, I'm guessing Tina's shoes had had an unfortunate altercation with the snow shovel peeking out from behind the passenger seat. You've got to give her credit for her aim, though—Tina's always been a crack shot when it comes to that kind of thing. She's the only person I've ever seen make a carni-val worker cry.

Barefoot, Tina flounced over to the margarita table and snatched up another drink, guzzling it as she glared at Principal Smoody.

"Look, no shoes," Ty said in a monotone. "Don't have to worry about that now."

"Nope," I agreed. Not that the monster was likely

to make an appearance anyway. It had seemed like such a huge threat a couple of hours before, but now it didn't even seem real. I'd never seen the lake look so dull.

The next couple of hours were boring beyond my wildest dreams. And Ty kept up a running monologue of every uninteresting event.

"Look, Señora Jenkins is dancing on that chair. Look, Sheriff Shifflett's talking to Amber again. Look at Principal Smoody suck down that fake margarita."

It wasn't what you would call a thrill-fest. The only one who was really happy was Mr. Boots. He was ankle deep in muck, sniffing every inch of path, and peeing occasionally on the hem of his skirt. He was in heaven. I let out the Flexi leash as far as it could go and scanned the shoreline again. Nothing.

Just when I thought I couldn't bear to hear another Spanish folk song, Señora Jenkins turned off the music, stood up, and clicked some little finger cymbals together. It was very dramatic. I felt like applauding. I think I had started to go flippy.

"I think they're going to crown the Prom Queen," I said, drawing circles in the dirt with a stick.

"Great." Ty's eyes weren't even open anymore. "A Tina vs. Amber catfight. Me-ow." He hissed and made a halfhearted clawing motion in the air. "Want to head out after that? That gummy thing's not going to show. I bet it's scared of the lights."

"Probably." I nodded. "I'll reel Mr. Boots in." I chucked the stick into the lake and grabbed the handle of the Flexi leash. The last time I'd checked Mr. Boots, he'd been sniffing a dandelion growing by the side of the path and sneezing. I should be getting him home anyway. All that pollen wasn't good for his sinuses.

"Hey, Mr. Boots!" I whispered, tugging on the leash a little.

It was like I'd hooked the big one. The Flexi leash suddenly went so taut I could barely keep my grip on it.

"What the—," I said, peering into the darkness.

That's when Mr. Boots screamed.

CHAPTER 14

I'D NEVER HEARD A SCREAM LIKE THAT BEFORE in my life. It was like an icicle had fallen and stabbed me right through the heart. A scream like that was big enough to rip Mr. Boots in two.

I looked up toward the end of the Flexi leash and almost screamed myself. Looming over the water, bigger than I'd ever imagined it could be, was the gummy thing. And suctioned right on the end of its tentacle was Mr. Boots.

I don't know where that thing had come from, but that gummy tentacle was suctioned firmly to Mr. Boots's gold lamé butt. Mr. Boots was hanging upside down, his little skirt falling over his head and his hind feet flailing wildly. I wanted to jump up and pull Mr. Boots right off that sucker, but I didn't dare. I felt so ashamed of myself. I was nothing but a huge chicken.

Tears sprang to my eyes. I couldn't believe this was happening. Not Mr. Boots. I didn't want it to dissolve Mr. Boots. Luckily, I wasn't the only one.

"Arlie, what the hell are you doing here?" Tina's voice rang strong and clear across the lake. It was like she was the only living person on a platform filled with statues, everybody else was so still. Señora Jenkins had frozen mid cymbal crash, and a fake margarita dangled forgotten in Bunny Smoody's hand. They all were mesmerized by the thing in the lake. Tina took a swig of fake margarita and marched up to the railing.

"I—I—," I squeaked, trying to make words. I knew I'd done it before. But for some reason my mouth wasn't working. I was having a hard time tearing my eyes away from the monster. Ty wasn't in any better shape than I was.

He had barely even breathed since Mr. Boots's scream, but his eyes were following every swing of the tentacle.

"Tell that roach to get away from Mr. Boots," Tina bellowed across the lake. I squeaked again. It was not my finest moment.

Tina rolled her eyes at me and turned to Principal Smoody. "Hey! Authority figure. That thing has my dog. Do something," she demanded.

Principal Smoody looked at the monster, put his hand on his stomach, and promptly fainted.

It would've been funny if it hadn't been so awful. Mr. Boots didn't have that much time. That gummy thing worked too fast. I scanned the crowd on the platform, hoping to see Sheriff Shifflett saunter forward and blow the gummy thing away. But nobody moved. Sheriff Shifflett was nowhere to be seen.

I tried desperately to figure out how long it had taken that frog to melt away. But I couldn't remember, and even if I could've, I wasn't sure how long Mr. Boots had been up there. But that frog had started dissolving almost instantly, and for some reason Mr. Boots was still there.

"It's going to dissolve him," I managed to croak. My voice sounded thin and weak as it echoed across the silent lake.

Miraculously, Tina seemed to hear me. "Do what?"

"Dissolve him."

Tina snorted. "Like hell it will. Hey!" she yelled at the monster. The monster was too busy suctioning Mr. Boots to respond.

"HEY!" Tina yelled again. "Let go of the dog!" The twinkling lights from the platform reflected against Mr. Boots's gold lamé dress as he struggled and made him look like a canine disco ball. I couldn't believe I'd been so careless with the little guy. I hadn't planned on using him as a decoy before. I just wanted him to have some fun.

I stared hard at Mr. Boots, disco edition, and at the tentacle grabbing onto the fabric of his dress. And suddenly I knew what was different.

"It's the gold lamé," I whispered. "Tammy's belt, the one they found, it was gold lamé too. The gold lamé, Ty, it can't dissolve the gold lamé." Forget everything I ever said about gold lamé being tacky. I was wrong—it's the best fabric in the world.

On the platform, Tina was quickly slipping into her enraged mode. She didn't do it often, but anybody who'd seen it once never wanted to see it again. I'd been on the receiving end a couple of times, and let me tell you, it'll blast the hair right off your head if you don't watch out.

"HEY! Let him GO!" Tina screamed so loud she almost made ripples on the water. Then, eyes narrowed in rage, she flung her plastic margarita glass across the lake. It was a good throw, and it's a teeny lake, but honestly, it was pathetic. Like a fake margarita was going to have any effect. I was almost embarrassed for her.

The drink splashed onto the monster and absorbed instantly, just like the weed killer had the day before. But the cup was a different story. The rim of the plastic cup caught the monster squarely in the middle. And it stuck.

I blinked hard. The plastic cup just stuck there like it was embedded for a couple of seconds before falling away. As it tumbled into the lake, I couldn't believe what it had done. Right in the center of the gummy thing's middle was a circle.

That cup had branded the monster, just as surely as if it had been a hot poker. But for the life of me I didn't see how. It was just your standard-issue plastic drugstore cup. Nothing special about it. Except one thing.

My feet were moving before my brain even finished the thought. I knew what to do. I knew how we could kill the monster.

"Ty, the car!" I screamed, racing off toward Trey's car, with Ty fast on my heels. I was just climbing into the front seat when Tina started to laugh. Not just a fake laugh either, but huge gales of uncontrollable laughter. Very slowly, every head turned to watch her as she bounced up and down in mirth. Either Tina had figured it out too, or she was totally flipping out. I didn't want to speculate; I was too busy trying to figure out how to start the damn thing.

This is probably the time to mention that no, I don't

know how to drive. But I wasn't going to let a little thing like that stop me. The keys were right there in the ignition, and that's all I needed. I hit the gas and lurched off in the direction of the lake, stopping for only a second to let Ty climb into the backseat.

"The salt, Ty!" I shouted, hitting the gas again. Driving skills didn't matter, all that mattered was getting to that gummy thing before it finished off Mr. Boots. We didn't have much time left, I could tell—little wisps of smoke had started coming from Mr. Boots's hindquarters. I didn't know how much longer that dress of his would hold out. I was lucky it was just a straight shot—no fancy driving maneuvers required. We were home free. Or we would've been if that tree stump hadn't been in the way.

Apparently, when your car is in a tailspin, you can't really steer. Which luckily isn't that important when your target is a lake. We found the lake no problem, skidding to a stop when we were a few feet in, just as Tina waded up to the car.

You've got to hand it to Tina, she really knows how

to put on a show. She'd hiked up her skirt, launched herself over the platform railing, and waded over to meet us before the wheels had even stopped spinning.

Ty leaned so far out of the window I thought he'd fall out, and heaved the rock salt to Tina. She caught it and headed the last few feet toward that gummy thing. There was no doubt in my mind, this was going to work. Everybody knows Tina kills roaches.

"Don't like the margaritas, do you, Roach? A little salty for you?" Tina gave the monster a slow, triumphant smile, and I swear, if a gummy monster can look uncertain, this one did.

With all her strength and one last evil smile, Tina heaved the entire bag of rock salt onto its slimy body.

I wouldn't say I have a weak stomach, but what happened next really turned it upside down. That salt burned into the monster's slimy skin like hot matches into styrofoam. The monster shook for a second, and then the vacuum grip it had on Mr. Boots completely lost its suction. Mr. Boots fell face-first into the lake and immediately dragged himself out and under a bush. I buried my face in my hands, practically sobbing with relief. I would've missed the grossest part if Ty hadn't elbowed me in the ribs. I'm still not sure whether to thank him or throttle him.

The air suddenly filled with a low hissing sound, and I looked up just in time to see the monster start to shake and shrivel. He was melting away right before our eyes, each burn hole getting bigger and bigger. It was just like the frog, except a thousand times worse. Because that gummy thing didn't just quietly dissolve. It exploded into an oozing mass of liquid, spewing globs of slime everywhere.

By the time it was finished, everything was covered with thick puddles of slime. It was repulsive. It was like living in a Kleenex in the aftermath of a sneeze.

Tina didn't seem to care, though. She was completely coated in brownish goop, but I've never seen her look happier. She tossed the empty salt bag over her shoulder and waded over to where me and Ty were huddled in the car.

"Let's go find the little squirt," she said, grinning.

We all waded over to the bushes on the other side of the river, and I dragged Mr. Boots out from under his bush. He took one look at Tina and attached himself to her like he had Velcro paws. The whole back of his gold lamé dress had dissolved away, but I didn't mind being mooned. I was just glad the little guy was okay.

"You realize I'm going to have to kill all of you when we get home," Tina said, making coochie motions under Mr. Boots's chin.

I laughed. "Better you than that thing."

Tina threw a big blob of slime at me and started back across the lake to the platform. "I told you not to worry, Arlie. I can handle things." She made a face at me and climbed back onto the platform. "Well?" she said. "Aren't you coming?"

That was all the invitation we needed. Me and Ty wiped the slime out of our eyes and left the quivering remains behind as we waded across the lake and up onto the platform.

CHAPTER 15

BY THE TIME ME AND TY MADE IT UP ON THE platform, Mr. Boots was sitting next to the margarita machine, totally nude. I know he's a dog, but still, I was shocked.

"I can't believe I made him wear that stupid dress," Tina was saying, viciously shredding what was left of the gold lamé outfit. "It practically killed him."

"Well, I would blame that on the monster," said Ty, stepping over Principal Smoody, who was lying on his stomach with his eyes squeezed shut, groaning. Bunny and Señora

Jenkins stopped fanning the principal and glared at Ty, but he was too busy eyeing the fake margaritas to notice. They did look pretty good.

"Are you kidding?" Tina squealed. "The way the lights were reflecting off of this thing? That roach would never have taken a second look at him if he hadn't been so stylish." She shook the dress and attempted to drop-kick it into the lake. It fluttered about a foot before Trey accidentally smushed it under his mucky wingtip. "It honed in on poor Mr. Boots like he was wearing a blue bug light on his butt. I'm serious, that is it for Mr. Boots and clothes. From now on, he's strictly a nudist."

I actually thought that was pretty unfair, considering the gold lamé dress was what had saved Mr. Boots's life, but he looked so happy being naked, I wasn't about to spoil his fun.

I just nodded agreeably and poured fake margaritas for me and Ty instead. I figured we'd earned them.

"Is it gone yet?" Amber Vanderklander popped up from behind the platform. She'd managed to escape the hail of slime, but it looked like she'd taken a dive head-first into a scrubby bush instead.

"Tina killed it," Trey bragged, putting his arm around Tina's shoulder. "She's a killer." Mr. Boots gagged and licked the margarita nozzle. I pretended not to notice. He'd had a tough day.

"Oh, good." Amber stood up and wiped the stray leaves off her mud-smeared satin skirt. "It's okay, you can come out now. Tina Jacobs killed it," she called back over her shoulder as she crawled up onto the platform.

Sheriff Shifflett poked his head up a second later and glanced around, wearing his favorite law-enforcement frown. The macho act wasn't quite cutting it, though. It's hard to be a tough guy with a caterpillar in your hair. "All clear down here, kids. Nothing to worry about, just some minor wildlife issues. I've cleared the area." He climbed up onto the platform and hooked his thumbs in his belt.

Nobody said a word. Sheriff Shifflett was never going to live this down.

Tina handled the situation like a pro, though. She discreetly pried Mr. Boots's lips from around the nozzle of the margarita machine and filled one of the plastic cups. "Drink, Sheriff?" I think she may have even batted her eyelashes. I wouldn't put it past her.

Sheriff Shifflett wiped his forehead on his sleeve. "Don't mind if I do. Thanks, missy." Apparently, he didn't notice the spit string leading from Mr. Boots's mouth to the nozzle. He actually looked touched. I don't know how touched he would've been if he'd realized he was drinking a glassful of dog slobber. Sheriff Shifflett downed the fake margarita to a chorus of muffled giggles just as Principal Smoody decided to show signs of life again. He lurched to his feet and staggered over to a chair near Carla Tate, huge sweat stains forming under his armpits. Bunny hovered beside him, blowing heavily on his face the whole time. Señora Jenkins looked slightly disgusted by the whole thing.

Principal Smoody shook his head. "I can't believe it! That fish was enormous."

Carla raised an eyebrow. "Fish?"

Principal Smoody gave a small sob. "It was huge. So huge."

Carla shrugged and grinned at Tina. "That's right, Principal Smoody. Such a big, scary fish." She patted him on the head like he was a puppy.

Smoothing her hair, Señora Jenkins marched back over to the tape player, obviously ready to get back to business. I groaned. I was suffering from a severe Lionel Richie overdose. Luckily, Donna Cavillari and Amber Vanderklander saw what she was planning and headed off disaster.

"It's okay, Señora Jenkins," Donna said with a smile, carefully blocking the tape player while Amber pulled an iPod out of her pocketbook. Señora Jenkins wavered anxiously. You could tell she had a serious case of disco fever.

Donna patted her on the shoulder. "We'll take care of this. You just rest." Amber triumphantly plugged an iPod adapter into the tape player, and the two of them happily got to work making the prom a more dance-friendly place.

The prom pretty much kicked back into gear after that, except with better music. And once Señora Jenkins had recovered from the shock of losing the tape wars, she decided to go ahead and hold the elections for Prom Queen and King. No surprise, Tina was elected by a landslide. Even Amber voted for her, which came as a shock, since she'd been campaigning pretty hard herself. Apparently vanquishing deadly gummy monsters can get you places.

The big surprise came with the vote for Prom King. Trey was the odds-on favorite, so it was quite an upset when Mr. Boots took the crown in a landslide. Trey was a gracious loser, although he did suggest that Mr. Boots's victory had something to do with his lack of clothing. I think he was heard using the term "butt naked." Mr. Boots was not amused.

Trey wasn't half as surprised as Mom and Dad were, though. You should've seen their faces when Tina came home from the prom with me and Mr. Boots in tow.

"We weren't waiting up, I swear we just—Tina, your hair! What happened?" Mom squealed, totally forgetting her rehearsed spiel. "Arlie, what are you doing with—Mr. Boots! You're naked!" Dad had to get her a sedative.

Mom had calmed down enough by the next morning to read the newspaper article that appeared in the local paper. The headline read LARGE CARP DISRUPTS JUNIOR-SENIOR PROM, and Principal Smoody was quoted extensively. He described the monster as a large, six-foot carp that splashed many unfortunate promgoers. Principal Smoody added that the large fish was quickly subdued and no one was injured. Sheriff Shifflett was quoted as saying that the person who had killed the fish was clearly in violation of state fishing ordinances, but that under the circumstances, he wasn't planning to prosecute. I'm sure Tina was so relieved. The real story came out a few days later in the *Daily Squealer*, complete with blurry cell phone pictures. It was right on the money, so

of course nobody believed it. It was written as an anony-
mous article, so no one knew how they'd gotten so much
information, but if you ask me, the Spanish phrases and
constant glowing references to Lionel Richie were sort
of a tip-off.

Sheriff Shifflett's display really impressed the kids at
school, let me tell you. Even without the *Daily Squealer*
article, word spread like wildfire about how he'd wimped
out at the prom. Even Amber wouldn't have anything to
do with him.

Last I heard, Sheriff Shifflett was dead last in the
polls for re-election. The Happy Hog statue down at the
Happy Mart had more votes than he did. I'm not kidding, either.

As for me and Ty, we decided to help the new science
teacher, Mrs. Barnard, with the cleanup project at the
lake. She was able to trace the mutation problem to a local
chemical plant, and they're funding the cleanup. Principal
Smoody convinced her not to mention mutations in her
report, except in regard to five-legged frogs and fish with

feet, but that was enough. Lake Heather's definitely going to be an awesome place when we get through.

That's not the whole reason we signed up, though. We had one last mission before we could put the whole gummy monster incident behind us. And it wasn't going to be pretty.

People always say that the best thing to do is get right back on the horse, right? Well, me and Ty had pretty much moved on, but Mr. Boots was having issues. All you had to do was say the word "lake" in front of him and he instantly transformed from a joyful canine nudist into a quivering pile of Chihuahua goo. And believe me, nobody wants to see that.

The lake was still cordoned off because there was a lot of cleanup left to do, but once we had permission from Mrs. Barnard, we put our plan into action. I felt kind of bad about it at first, but looking back, Ty was right—there's no way Mr. Boots would have come willingly. Tying him to the skateboard with a bungee cord was a good safety move. Although I still think the tiny blindfold was a bit much. I had the feeling he thought we were planning to stand him in front of a wall and offer him a cigarette.

Once we got him back to the scene of the crime, we untied his little paws and whipped off the blindfold.

"Here you go, Mr. Boots," Ty said, waving the blindfold around like he was in some lakeside rhythmic gymnastics competition. "See? Nothing to be afraid of! No monsters, no stinky slime, nothing! It's just a lake."

Mr. Boots flared his nostrils, looked around, and promptly went into goo mode. So much for the plan.

I opened my mouth to say something reassuring, but just as I did, I caught a glimpse of something out of the corner of my eye that stopped me cold. Something moving in the reeds by the edge of the water. Something gummy.

I felt sick to my stomach. This could not be happening.

"Uh, Ty?" I pointed into the reeds. "How long did Mrs. Barnard say before the lake's all clean?"

Ty frowned. "Soon, I think." He peered closely at the reeds where I was pointing, and then whipped his head around to gape at me.

I'd wanted to think it was a trick of the light, but Ty's reaction pretty much cinched it. A mini version of the gummy monster had blobbed out of the lake and was crawling quickly in the direction of Ty's shoe.

"Oh man, Ty," I said, staring at the thing. It was just like the big one, except this one was about the size of a fun-size candy bar. "Hopefully real soon."

The thing was about a foot away from Ty when Mr. Boots made his move. That tiny version of his enemy was all the therapy he needed. He instantly leaped to his feet and launched himself at the gummy monster, grabbing it in his mouth and whapping it from side to side against the ground, a maniacal gleam in his eye. Then he spat it into the reeds and leaped onto it again, pummeling it with his front feet like it was a dog-size punching bag.

"Man, he's good." Ty looked impressed.

It became obvious pretty fast that Mr. Boots was a

secret fan of professional wrestling, because he had the moves down pat. And wearing his rhinestone collar, he even kind of looked the part. I'm thinking he could get job offers.

As good as he was, though, Mr. Boots was still a Chihuahua and basically a wuss at heart. The gummy monster seemed a little shaken, but after struggling out from between Mr. Boots's paws, it kept on its path toward us.

Ty shook his head. "Man, Arlie. What do we do?"

I stared at it for a second, and it hit me.

"No biggie." I grinned at Ty. Then I lifted up my clunky size seven and aimed it right at the little sucker.

"Tina's not the only one with killing shoes."

THE DAILY SQUEALER

TREMBLING TOWER OF TERROR PETRIFIES PROMGOERS

By an Unidentified Witness

It was a warm, pleasant evening on Lake Heather, and happy promgoers were swaying to the serene vocal stylings of the incomparable LIONEL RICHIE. But next on the agenda: TERROR.

Out of the lake, towering twenty feet in the air, was a putrid, festering, gooey hulk, threatening to spoil the happy high school memories of countless students by crushing their bones, hopes, and dreams. But never fear, three unlikely heroes were on hand to save the day. And who were these heroes? Three children and a Chihuahua.

Cleverly using their tiny canine as a decoy, the children lured the beast out of hiding. Wearing a protective garment designed to both allure and repel the monster, the tiny dog, known only as MR. BOOTS, lunged at the creature, firmly attaching himself to the creature's appendage by his behind. While the creature attempted to destroy his tiny attacker, the three children went to work to destroy the beast.

Driving the ambush vehicle? ARLENE JACOBS, junior high vigilante, aided by TYRONE PARKER, weapons expert. As their decoy cleverly distracted the beast, JACOBS and PARKER drove into the lake in an incredible display of stunt driving that would have been perfection itself if accompanied by the incredible sounds of "All Night Long." Waiting for the vehicle was the third hero, one TINA JACOBS, exterminator, who dealt the deadly blow by covering the blobby beast with a shower of rock salt.

As horrified and terrified promgoers, chaperones, and language experts watched in horror, the beast exploded into a gooey mass of terror.

Celebrations ensued, and MR. BOOTS shed his protective garment, as distinctive in its way as the white suit worn by MR. RICHIE in the glorious first years of his solo career. But reactions were mixed. Although all agreed that they were indebted to the fearless heroes, some students were dismayed by their methods. "I'm never going to get this dress clean," said one unidentified student. "And it's real polyester satin."

SIGHTING OF A YELLOW-BELLIED SHIFFLETT: STUDENTS SAY HE LEFT THEM TO DIE

I WAS FRAMED!
MAN KNOWN AS THE WALKER SUES CITY AFTER FALSE ARREST

SECRETS
OF SHERIFF SHIFFLETT: LIFTS AND GRECIAN FORMULA?

WE WANT THAT DOG!
K9 UNITS NATIONWIDE WOO ELUSIVE MR. BOOTS

CHEMICAL PLANT CONFESSES:
OUR DUMPING CREATED A MONSTER!

THE
CURSE
OF
CUDDLES
MCGEE

*CAN YOU STOP AN ANGRY PET THAT'S
COME BACK FROM THE GRAVE?*

By Emily Ecton

While poking around their neighborhood, mystery-solving, swamp-monster-fighting middle-graders Arlie and Ty discover a buried coffee can filled with the bones of a hamster and the handwritten curse (on glittery unicorn notepaper) from his home-schooled owner, Mandy:

HERE LIES CUDDLES MCGEE. A CURSE UPON THOSE WHO DISTURB HIS GRAVE.

The fact that the *i* in "lies" is topped with a heart doesn't make them any less scared, especially when the obese, angry, and undead Cuddles comes back to life and starts trashing the town.

Once again, it's up to Arlie, Ty, and the fashionably dressed Chihuahua Mr. Boots to save the town from destruction, reanimated-dead-hamster style.

COMING SOON!